Don't stop! don't die! his mind raged. *Not this close to freedom!*

Colonel Alex Bradford charged through the dense undergrowth as if the hounds of hell were after him. His heart pounded like a berserk jackhammer. As he hurtled along, lungs bursting, the only sounds he made were the whisper of parting branches. He had no idea how long he'd been a P.O.W.—Ten years? Fifteen? Bradford felt lightheaded. He wondered how much longer he could push on before he dropped...

M.I.A. HUNTER

JACK BUCHANAN

A JOVE BOOK

M.I.A. HUNTER

A Jove Book/published by arrangement with
the author

PRINTING HISTORY
Jove edition/January 1985

ISBN: 0-515-08068-3

Jove books are published by The Berkley Publishing Group,
200 Madison Avenue, New York, N.Y. 10016. The words
"A JOVE BOOK" and the "J" with sunburst are trademarks
belonging to Jove Publications, Inc.

PRINTED IN THE UNITED STATES OF AMERICA

"Go with us as we seek to defend the defenseless and to free the enslaved."

—from the "Special Forces Prayer"

M.I.A. HUNTER

Prologue

Xieng Khouang Province, Laos

Home.

It was all he could think of.

In another twenty-four hours Corporal Ky Dac, a regular in the North Vietnamese Army, would be home in the suburbs of Hanoi, joyfully reunited, if only for a week-long furlough, with his friends and family.

Ky Dac wished there were some way he could will the time to fly faster so he could be gone that much sooner from this desolate hellhole in the mountainous rain forest of eastern Laos that had been his duty station for this past year, since his mandatory induction into the army at age sixteen.

It was almost dawn. The darkness was muggy, oppressive. The only sounds to be heard by the young sentry, as he patrolled his rounds, were the symphony of nightlife— bats, birds, monkeys, insects everywhere. This was the least populated section of the country. Laos wasn't as pretty as Ky's home in Vietnam. For one thing, there was a rainless summer here and the foliage held more brown than green.

Hardwood trees and some pine grew to within five feet of the eight-foot-high bamboo fence that was the perimeter of this small prison subcamp in the middle of nowhere, utilized by the army for the interrogation and detention of special prisoners.

After his week's leave, Ky would return to this duty for another year of service. But a week would be adequate, at least, he knew, to remind himself of the world that existed beyond this secluded clearing amid the ever-encroaching elements where a soul could go mad *if* one allowed oneself to forget that other world—the real world.

For the Americans imprisoned here, of course, this *was* their world. All of it. And Ky Dac had seen many lose their sanity. Suicides, yes.

Yet only two of the Americans had died in the year Ky had been stationed here, one a suicide, one of starvation.

The American prisoners seemed a breed apart. Their lives a never-ending hell, these men grew more stoic with each long, passing year of their captivity.

The American P.O.W.'s at this camp were among those lost souls listed as missing in action by their own country. For the last ten years these miserable devils had been shunted about Vietnam and Laos, from camp to camp, until now they functioned as slave labor at this small installation established some years ago, when much of Laos had been utilized as a staging area for the Vietnamese invasion of Cambodia.

Ky often marveled that the brass in Hanoi even remembered this out-of-the-way camp where he had the misfortune to be stationed. Yet they must have remembered. In twenty-four hours Ky would be on his way home . . .

Ky saw that something was wrong when he was within ten paces of the cages where the American P.O.W.'s were kept.

The cages were several feet off the ground, mounted on upright logs, and were barely illuminated by a lamp across the compound, near the thatch-roofed huts of the officers and guard personnel. The cages, or cells, were ten feet square, built of bamboo poles that had been nailed and tied together with rope. The cages were roofed with bark and leaves, the door of each cage secured with a heavy chain and padlock.

One of the cage doors was open!

Ky Dac stopped thinking about home.

The sentry swung around his Soviet-made AK-47 assault rifle from where it had been riding strapped over his shoulder. He advanced cautiously on the cages.

There were four prisoner cages in a row, a dozen feet in from the fenced perimeter. Ky Dac could discern the shadowy figures of the other three prisoners, supposedly asleep, weary from their long days of harsh labor and the brutality of the day guards.

But yes, the middle cage was vacant!

A prisoner was missing!

Ky mentally groped for the name of this prisoner even as he drew nearer to the cage to confirm what he was already sure of.

Bradford. That was the man's name. Colonel Alex Bradford.

Ky glanced frantically about. There was no sign of the missing prisoner. The young soldier felt his throat go dry. These prisoners were his responsibility. He had been on guard duty since midnight, he and one other man, and the prisoners were in Ky's sector of the compound. Yet he'd heard nothing. Ky hoped fervently that this would not endanger his furlough. He must alert Captain Chong immediately.

The sentry half-turned toward the huts across the clear-

ing. A flurry of movement engulfed him out of the gloom.
Ky somehow sensed the striking blow an instant before it
connected with the base of his skull. Then everything went
black for him. The sentry pitched to the ground, unconscious, without making a sound.

Colonel Alex Bradford charged through the dense
undergrowth of vegetation as if the hounds of hell were after
him, which indeed they were.

He'd shed his crude tire-tread sandals. Bare feet propelled him along across the caked red earth. He was clad
in a soiled shirt and grimy U.S. fatigues that had long ago
been torn away to just above the knees.

He had to keep shaking his head to toss off salty sweat
that stung his eyes like hot needles, blinding him from time
to time as he ran. But he did not stop running.

He would make it!

His heart pounded against his ribcage and in his ears like
a berserk jackhammer. He dashed madly through the forest
with the silence and speed of a cat. The only sounds he
made were the whisper of parting branches as he hurtled
along, and his ragged breathing that seemed too loud to
him, but which he could not control, gasping with the effort
of this long haul, from not being in shape. His years of
imprisonment had taken their toll. He had no idea how long
he'd been a P.O.W.—Ten years? Fifteen? Bradford felt
lightheaded. He wondered how much longer he could push
on before he dropped.

You have to make it! his mind screamed. *Stop and you're
dead!* Chong would kill him by slow inches.

The eastern sky was tinged with the first pink traces of
dawn.

The running man felt the sweat that bathed him all over
grow clammy with a new fear that suddenly gripped him.

He had expected to find a river; he thought it might be

the Mae Nam Mun, a tributary of the Mekong, that he knew flowed eastward, less than three kilometers from the Viet prison camp.

But there was no sign of the river.

Was he lost?

He charged on. *Go, go, go!* his mind raged. His heart pumped even faster. *Don't stop! Don't die! Not this close to freedom!*

These seven-thousand-foot mountains were deadly frontier, Bradford knew. In addition to the Viet military outposts, often manned by troops dependent on terrorizing and pillaging Laotian villages for their food, there were also gangs of wandering cutthroat hill bandits as well as hungry, desperate refugees trying to reach Thailand, and the ever-present patrols of the feared Pathet Lao, the Communist military force that supposedly ruled these highlands.

But once he reached that river, he would be all right. He could move southward toward Thailand. He could still survive in the jungle on his own. He knew he could. It hadn't been that long since his intensive training at Bragg. Well, okay, maybe it had been a while. Sometimes he felt as if he had known no other existence but the slave labor and the bamboo cages and the taunting, torturing guards and officers, as if everything before that had been only a dream now barely remembered. But Alex Bradford would not admit defeat. Hell no! Not with the sentry's AK-47 gripped in his hands and the soaring quest in his heart and soul that drove his pumping legs onward.

He *would* make it.

Once he reached that river, he could move along it until he found a trail or commandeered a peasant's sampan. He would travel by night, mostly, in an appropriated native outfit. He would reach Thailand. The Free World. He would return to the land of the living! And he would return with help for his buddies—Mandrell, Wilcox, Dermeer—who were still back at the camp. He would return to take vengeance on the camp's bastard commandant, Captain Chong.

Bradford owed Chong a very special blood debt. Alex had witnessed two of his buddies' deaths in the past month: Clayton from starvation, Buford when the poor slob just couldn't take it anymore and disemboweled himself with a sharp piece of bamboo in the middle of the compound while Alex screamed at him not to do it, and the guards stood and watched, some of them pointing and laughing. Chong had watched the awful act from the doorway of his hut, with those snake eyes gleaming and a bemused smile on his thin lips.

You'll die, Chong, sang Bradford's mind. *I'll come back and things will be set right. But first—Christ!—first I've got to get away. Get free. Bring help. To my family. Sweet Christ, my family! Nora and the kids. Dear God, let me make it—*

It was a chance in a million that had gotten him this far from the prison torture camp. The kid soldier on night guard duty—Ky was the boy's name, the only partly humane guard in the bunch—had seemed preoccupied when he locked up Alex and the other Americans late last night while talking to another sentry about his anticipation of an upcoming furlough that soldier Dac was to embark on when last night's duty was ended. Alex had fallen into sleep, or the fitful discomfort that passed for it in the cage, listening to the young sentries talk. He awoke sometime during the night to find that his mosquito net had slipped. He was being mauled by insects. In turning to swat them away and replace the net, Bradford's elbow had bumped against the door of his cage and the door had swung open.

Ky Dac had damn well had something else on his mind!

Alex slipped from his bamboo cage and checked the padlocks on the other three cages. The guard had not repeated his fuckup. The cages of Mandrell, Wilcox, and

Dermeer were securely locked as usual.

The other three P.O.W.'s quickly came awake. During the hurried, whispered conference that followed, it was decided that Bradford would make a break for it, to get help. One man alone could travel fast and true.

Mandrell, Wilcox, and Dermeer played possum when the young sentry returned on his rounds. Bradford popped the kid and grabbed his AK and extra ammo, then searched Ky for the key to the other cages. The key wasn't on the guard; it had probably been returned to Chong in case the commandant took it upon himself to "interrogate" one of the American P.O.W.'s as he often liked to do when he was drunk. The interrogations generally consisted of little more than the captain insulting or spitting on a prisoner, then perhaps urinating on him. But it could be worse—and it had been worse. The missing joint of Bradford's right index finger was proof of what Chong was capable of.

Alex had set out on his own. To have searched the camp for the key, even if the other three did have weapons to fight with when they were freed, would only have ended in the death of all four outnumbered P.O.W.'s. The other three prisoners had urged Bradford to hurry on his way before he was discovered.

It was daylight now.

They would be tracking him soon, Bradford knew, if they weren't already. *Where's that damn river?* He *had* to get out. He had to tell the world—a world that didn't even know that Alex Bradford and those other U.S. soldiers existed! Why should the Viet government admit to M.I.A.'s like them, at the expense of losing a lifetime of free slave labor?

Bradford knew he would stand and fight if it came to that. He would kill himself before he went back to that hellhole camp. But they wouldn't catch him. He *would* make it. *I'm coming home, Nora.* He was almost delirious with the thought but he pushed on, running running running.

The sweat was in his eyes, blinding him, and he did not see the ankle-high twist of vine that tripped him, spilling him forward. The violent green of the jungle seemed to reach out to strangle him. His forehead struck a half-buried rock. The green became black as Colonel Alex Bradford lost consciousness.

Ky Dac was yanked from the dark womb of unconsciousness by boots jabbing him painfully in the ribs. The sentry forced his eyes open to find himself lying on his back on the ground near the P.O.W. cages.

The first metallic light of day cast Ky's surroundings in a ghostly illumination that clearly showed the one empty cage with the yawning door. The young sentry abruptly recalled what had happened.

Sergeant Binh was kicking him awake.

Ky realized with a sinking feeling that he was in the worst trouble of his life.

"Wake up! Wake up, scum!" Binh was barking, over and over. "Answer our questions! Where is your prisoner?"

Captain Chong stood next to the sergeant. Ky saw that the three remaining American P.O.W.'s were awake in their cages, watching the scene. The other guards and personnel stood in a half-circle behind Chong and Binh, also watching.

Ky sat up, remaining on the ground. He stared wide-eyed at Chong and Binh, who towered above him.

"I was attacked!"

The sentry barely recognized his own voice.

"What time did it happen?" demanded Binh. "How long has the prisoner been gone?"

"I—I checked the time just before someone hit me," gasped Ky. "It could have been no later than oh-six-hundred hours."

Binh delivered another kick, particularly vicious.

"You were thinking of your furlough, damn you," he rasped. The sergeant turned to Dhong, indicating the sentry cowering at their feet. "What shall we do with this one, Captain?"

Chong was already turning back toward the main hut as he spoke.

"This man's failure is inexcusable," hissed the commandant. The pistol holstered at his hip seemed to leap into his fist.

"No!" screamed Ky.

Captain Chong aimed the pistol almost casually. When the barrel was less than twelve inches from Ky's shrieking face, the commandant triggered two rounds that burst the sentry's head into a froth of red and gray and flying chips of bone, and nailed Ky Dac to the ground amid a fast-spreading pool of blood that was as red as the clay beneath him.

"The prisoner's trail already grows cold," Chong snapped at Sergeant Binh. "Post guards with the prisoners who remain. You and your men and I will form a hunting party. This is the first prisoner escape ever from this camp. Colonel Bradford has not yet made good his escape. We *will* find him. Then he will pay."

Chapter One

Southern California

Mark Stone dropped from the high brick wall and landed without a sound.

A gibbous moon rode the cloudless night, but the shadows of the brick wall cloaked him until he darted like a silent wraith away from the wall toward the massive, vague shape of a structure on higher ground.

Conditions were far from ideal for a night test operation, but they would have to do. Other variables in this equation had already been set in motion, and Stone would not have aborted this action even if he could.

Stone was a big man, outfitted totally in combat black for a night hit. He had applied a black facial goo that camouflaged him completely in the darkness.

He was traveling light. A 9mm Beretta 93-R rode snugly in side leather below his left shoulder. Stilettos and other accessories were attached to his belt, as were a full complement of stun grenades.

He reached the shadows of the elegant but dated two-story stone house, pressing himself flat against the front wall of the structure, and angled toward the front entrance.

A sentry stood posted there, cradling an automatic assault rifle across his cocked left arm. The sentry was clad in student garb, a casual sweater and slacks, but there was nothing casual about the way he kept scanning the darkness in front of the looming building.

Stone sailed in from the side and zapped the guy with a judo chop before the sentry realized he was under attack.

Stone was halfway to the front door when another guard sauntered around the corner, strolling directly toward him.

Guard Number Two's eyes and nostrils flared in alarm as his rifle's muzzle rose toward the intruder.

Stone's right arm flashed outward from his combat utility belt. The sentry took a stiletto high in the chest and collapsed next to the first guard with barely a sound.

Stone stepped over the prone bodies, palming the Beretta. He cocked back his right foot and sent the front double oak doors of the house slamming inward off their hinges with a powerful kick. He entered the house low and fast, his left hand unhooking one of the stun grenades.

Three more sentries, all of them heavy with sidearms and automatic rifles, stood stationed around the closed door midway down the corridor. All three rifles tracked upward as one in Stone's direction, but Mark had already pulled the grenade's pin and was tossing the grenade in vital milliseconds that made all the difference.

Stone sensed another presence closing in on the threesome in the hallway from the opposite end of the corridor.

It was the powerful, bearlike figure of Hog Wiley, the ugliest man Mark Stone had ever known. Hog was a bearded, wild-haired behemoth of a "good old boy" from east Texas, a dirt-track racing driver with a disposition that favored demolition derbies. Hog was an expert wheelman with any vehicle, and was happiest in a fight, in a woman, or bathed in grease, working mechanic's magic on a dismantled engine. Wiley was the kind of go-for-broke wild-lifer who had already probably tried all three at once, or more than once. He also happened to be one of the five top combat-specialist mercs for hire, an expert in light weapons and a disciplined master of hand-to-hand combat. Hog had a gruff, raunchy, but honest quality about him that Stone enjoyed. But the big man could be sudden death in a fire-fight. Stone knew this from firsthand experience. He and Hog had served together in Nam.

The husky six-foot-plus Wiley lobbed a stun grenade of his own, just as Stone spotted him. Hog could float like a butterfly despite his size, but he always stung like a two-ton bee.

Stone and Hog covered their eyes with their arms against the blinding white flashes of the grenades. The blasts were loud, but for this particular operation ear plugs solved that problem.

The three sentries in the hallway caught the full effect of the double whammy that kicked them flailing backward against the walls.

Stone and Wiley closed in. Three well-placed chops finished the job on these guards. The two combat specialists then hurried toward the door these men had been guarding.

Stone went in first, with another kick that propelled another door inward from its hinges. Hog lumbered in behind him as backup, a long-barreled .357 looking like a toy in his hamlike right fist.

Another Stone ally, Terrance Loughlin, was at that moment dropping into the room from an overhead ventilation duct.

Loughlin was a red-haired British-version of Mark Stone; he had the same size and build as Mark, and like Mark, Loughlin handled his weapon as if it were an extension of himself. The Brit had served as a demolitions expert in the U.K.'s crack antiterrorist Special Air Service commando unit until his effectiveness was compromised during an embassy hostage rescue action, when a terrorist yanked away Loughlin's mask before he could blow the guy away. A news camera caught Loughlin's unmasked features for posterity, and for terrorist files, so he had been mustered out, albeit honorably, to become yet another ex-military man who hired himself out as a professional mercenary.

The Brit exile occasionally exhibited traces of bitterness for having been retired prematurely after his years of outstanding service, but Loughlin was melancholy by nature and it never interfered with his reputation as the best demo expert merc in the business. The tough Englishman had more than once proved his value to Mark Stone in tense combat situations.

Loughlin dropped to a springy crouch in front of Stone and Wiley without loosening his grip on the 9mm Ingram submachine gun he toted.

The three men then turned as one to look expectantly at the lone occupant of the room.

Carol Jenner rose from the armchair where she had been sitting. She clicked off the stopwatch she held.

"Sixty-three seconds, on the nose," she told them.

The tension in the room dissipated. Stone, Loughlin, and Wiley lowered their weapons.

Hog cursed colorfully.

"I don't get it. Where did we pick up three extra seconds?"

"My fault," said Mark. "I had to take out a sentry in front who wasn't supposed to be there."

"Fault, hell," Carol beamed. "That was still record time."

Big, beautiful, and tough, with a touch of class, blonde, blue-eyed Carol was proportioned like a midnight sex fantasy—everything the songwriters and poets have in mind when they talk about woman's magic and power. The knowledge that she was all of this and that she was all his because that was the way she wanted it, anytime *he* wanted it, did nothing to dull the warm quiver that Mark felt every time he saw her, like now. Carol was some kind of lady. She was Mark Stone's steady lover.

She joined the men as they walked from the room into a hallway littered with bodies that were slowly reviving themselves to life amid groans and grumbles and grudging admiration for the assault that had defeated them.

"Uh-oh," said Terrance Loughlin at Stone's side. "Visitors."

Two men stood at the end of the hall, blocking exit via the front double doorway. The big guy on the right faced Stone with hard eyes and a look that said he could handle himself anywhere. The smaller man who stood beside him was mousy, gripping a briefcase as if for protection.

"You folks have time to spare?" asked the big one in a steel-edged voice that said this was only a preliminary nicety; the hard punch would take a while, if it came at all this time.

Mark still held his Beretta in his right hand, aimed down at his side, but the pistol's magazine held only cartridges that fired red paint pellets to verify hits, as did the weapons of Loughlin and Wiley. But Stone was nonetheless prepared in case this confrontation, whatever it was, split the wrong way and exploded. He sensed that the same was true of the woman and two men who had fanned out behind him.

The air was electric.

"I.S.A.?" asked Stone.

The big guy flipped open a leatherbound folder and extended International Security Affairs credentials for Mark's inspection. The I.S.A. was parent organization to the Defense Security Assistance Agency, which dealt with the P.O.W./M.I.A. issue.

"Harker." The cold-eyed Fed pocketed the ID and nodded to the mousy guy alongside him. "This is Fred Derring."

Stoner recognized the name although he had never met Derring.

"Well, well. The chief counsel for Senator Ordway's subcommittee. Blow the whistle on any covert U.S. operations today, counselor?"

Derring bristled but stayed well behind Harker's bulk.

"See here, Stone. You can be resubpoenaed, you know. You're a licensed private investigator in this state. That does not give you the right to—"

"Balls," grumbled Hog Wiley. "Them politicians went over Sarge with a microscope. We're one hundred percent legal, and you dudes know it, and that's stuck right in your craw and you all can't do a damn thing about it, can you?"

Hog seemed to take a fair amount of amusement in this.

Stone told the mismatched Feds exactly what he'd told Ordway's subcommittee under oath during closed hearings earlier that year.

"I'm a private eye to make a living. What I do on my own time, and where I do it, is my business."

"Even when you illegally infiltrate foreign countries without U.S. authorization on paramilitary operations in search of P.O.W.'s that do not exist?" demanded Derring.

"Yeah, even then," grunted Mark. "Especially then."

"The official position of this government is that the Vietnam War is over. All P.O.W.'s and M.I.A.'s have been accounted for. Case closed, Stone."

Hog Wiley put into one word what Mark Stone was thinking.

"Bullshit," groused the big man. "I say we toss these cruds out on their ears, Sarge," he added.

Hog's patience with authority was nonexistent, but the big Fed, Harker, appeared unimpressed.

"Put your animal on a leash," he told Stone coolly. "Private investigators are licensed. Licenses can be pulled."

A little of the tension dissipated when another man walked over to them. The guy was one of the sentries from in front of the house, the one Mark had stilettoed on his way in. The man tugged the stiletto from his nylon-weave protective vest and handed it back to Stone.

"Good work, fellas," he said with a grin. "You guys are tops. We learn plenty from these exercises. All the guys in the precinct wish they could get in on it. Same time next week?"

Mark sheathed the stiletto and gave a thumbs-up sign to his opposite team leader.

"If we can, pal. Thanks."

The other man picked up on the scene then, and turned to stand shoulder-to-shoulder alongside Stone, warily facing the Feds.

"You guys need some help?" the team leader asked Mark.

"Not this time, Tony. It's cool. Thanks anyway."

The man paused long enough to make sure, then turned and went back down the hallway to help his teammates, all off-duty rookie cops, to their feet and out through the other door.

Derring's face pinched with distaste.

"A farm made into a course for survivalist war games. What a way for grown men to pass their time. Why not place a bit more faith in your government, Mr. Stone?"

"My government is responsible for allowing those P.O.W.'s to rot to death in 'Nam while we stand here talking," rasped Mark. He locked eyes with Harker. "If this is a bust, let's go. If it's a subpoena, serve it. Otherwise, move out of our way."

"Word on the merc grapevine is that you're going into the field again," said Harker. "Is that what this workout tonight is all about? Last-minute training?"

"I'll ask you politely one last time, because you do represent my government," said Mark, very softly. "Step aside."

"I say we take 'em apart for the bloody sport of it," grunted Loughlin.

"Guys, please—" began Carol.

Harker ignored the others. He glared at Mark.

"I lost a son in 'Nam. You make me think of what Jerry might've been like, Stone—if he'd come home alive. I know what you stand for and what you're trying to do. No one wants to see American GIs still held as prisoners of war. But you can't solve this issue with vigilante justice. The government is planning steps. But the only way to play it—for the sake of those P.O.W.'s, if they do exist—is by the damn rules."

"And what if the rules don't work?" Stone asked quietly. "What then, Harker?"

"We're not here to debate this issue," the mouse piped up almost primly from where he still stood, well behind Harker. "We are here to serve notice to you and your men, Stone, that you will be in very serious trouble if we do find proof that you're going over again."

"What Derring is trying to say is that you'll be resub-poenaed, I'll see that your private investigator's license is pulled, and I'll show you tricks to make a man miserable that you never thought of," said Harker.

"Fair enough," said Stone. "Now if you'll excuse us, gentlemen?"

Harker finally stepped out of the way. Derring receded with him.

Mark and his crew exited the house, into the night, and walked across the short distance to where their vehicles were parked.

"Stay at your contact numbers from here on out," Stone instructed Loughlin and Wiley in a whisper. "I'm connecting with our new client as soon as I get this goo off my face and change clothes. It'll go down anytime now."

"I'll take the bloody phone to bed with me," was the Englishman's parting shot. Loughlin strode off toward his sporty rental car.

"I'll be on tap if you need me, Sarge," grunted Wiley.

"I know you will. Thanks."

Stone watched Wiley amble off toward his Harley. Then Mark walked Carol over to her car, where he held the door open for her to slide in.

"It wasn't a good idea, you coming here tonight," he told her.

"Mark, I'll only be on the Coast for these two days." Lush, full lips curved into a smile that was pure Mona Lisa with spice. "And you know how I like to watch you work." The blonde smacked her lips appreciatively and her smile widened.

He grinned back at her. "I dig you too, lady. But what would Derring and Harker say if they recognized the woman I'm with as an intel processor at the Defense Department?"

"I can take care of myself."

"I know you can, but so can they. If Harker IDs you and your position at Defense, and learns that your brother was listed as M.I.A. during the war, then he won't have any trouble figuring out where I get my logistical intel before I head out on a mission. Those recon photos and maps come in real handy. Maybe they'll help me find your own brother someday. They've helped bring home several men already. Your role in this operation is too vital to endanger."

"You're right, of course," she said contritely. "I'll be more thoughtful in the future, Mark. We've all put in too much to throw it away now."

"I gotta go, Carol," he said, pulling her toward him.

"Be careful, honey."

There was time for a quick but soulful kiss, and Mark

Stone watched Carol drive away. Then he turned and walked toward his own vehicle, a Lancia. He could feel eyes watching his every move from somewhere in the darkness around him. He knew his mission had already begun.

Chapter Two

It took Stone all of ten minutes to lose the unmarked car that tailed him away from the survivalist game course. Mark had expected no less of Harker. He commenced evasive action the minute his northward drive took him to the outer reaches of suburbs at the very southern tip of the Los Angeles megalopolis.

Stone steered his Lancia with all the finesse at his command. Traffic was sparse at this late-night hour, but he played the winding residential streets for all they were worth, leading the tracking Impala on a spirited maze of hide-and-seek that ended with the Fed car still seeking while Stone resumed heading north for another ten minutes to Newport Beach, where he was scheduled to make initial contact with the woman who wanted to hire him.

Mark Stone had been a master sergeant in a Green Beret Special Forces unit stationed at Da Nang during the Vietnam War. His specialty had been covert actions of all kinds, usually involving hit-and-run, cross-border operations into Laos, Cambodia, and North Vietnam. He had gone through

extensive stateside training in all of the classic infiltration
techniques, including weapons, demolitions, hand-to-hand
combat, survival, paratroop training, and camouflage. Stone
had played a vital part in many of the most sensitive operations of that war, including the assassination of General
Nu Trang, which had significantly sabotaged the enemy's
infamous Tet Offensive.

Mark had the distinction of having served more tours of
duty in Indochina than any other Special Forces soldier, so
that by the time he left South Vietnam during the last days
of the fall of Saigon, the lean, muscular, six-foot-one penetration specialist knew that corner of the world better than
most soldiers at combat level. Stone was totally conversant
with the languages, people, politics, and terrain of that
exotic world of lush jungle and mountains and ancient civ-
ilizations and customs that flow uninterrupted from history
into the future. Stone particularly understood the very special conditions of combat that hedged the bets for a warrior's
survival in a green hell that had been ravaged by war and
grief since long before the time of Christ.

Since the pullout of U.S. troops from 'Nam, Mark had
been living stateside in the Southern California wasteland
of sun and sleaze, where he stayed in shape and had found
financial success working as a private detective for the fast-
lane Hollywood set.

Private-eyeing was a job to Stone, nothing more. He was
his own boss, with enough financial security to accommodate a beach house in Venice, California, and a quiet
personal life. But Stone's blue-gray eyes, which had seen
so much in war-torn 'Nam, could never lose the objective
cool of an outsider in smoggy, sinful L.A. Mark was ex-
tremely competent, but not terribly dedicated to his work
as a private investigator.

The only activity that gave meaning to the thirty-five-year-old ex-Green Beret's life was his "second job" as an M.I.A. hunter.

Mark returned periodically to Southeast Asia in search of American missing-in-action prisoners of war for the families of such men who hired him. Mark would also come back with *any* American he found being held prisoner during his specific missions.

Of necessity, Mark kept a very low profile. The most important condition that he always insisted upon from those who hired him was complete confidentiality. Mark did not advertise his services. The cover of Stone Investigative Consultants was perfect for potential clients who wished to contact him. That was how this nocturnal appointment with Nora Bradford had been arranged. Stone's potential clients never actually came to Stone's North Hollywood office, which he was certain was under government surveillance.

The contact point with Mrs. Bradford was a public parking lot adjacent to a stretch of beach, deserted at this hour, bathed in moonglow and caressed by the eternal lapping of the Pacific.

Mark steered his Lancia into the parking area and braked alongside the only other car in sight, a late-model Camaro. He left his car and approached the other vehicle. He leaned down and looked into the car from the open window on the passenger side.

A woman sat behind the Camaro's steering wheel, nervously puffing on a cigarette, obviously waiting.

"Mrs. Bradford?"

"Yes. Mr. Stone?"

"That's right."

"Please get in."

He did. In the brief illumination from the car's overhead light he saw that Nora Bradford was an attractive brunette in her early forties. He also noted a strained tightness around the woman's mouth and in her eyes, and in the jerky concentration of her smoking.

Stone had come to recognize these as standard symptoms of those who had only very recently learned shocking good news, immediately overshadowed by the even more shocking truth concerning the bureaucratic bumbling of their government, before being forced to resort to other channels that had led this woman to a moonlit beach in Southern California at what she probably, and quite rightly, perceived as her last chance, her last stop before giving up altogether on an ephemeral hope that had at first ignited so much joy and been almost real enough to touch.

"Mr. Stone, your name was given to me by Mrs. Virgil Shumway of Fort Worth," she told him without preamble. "I was put in touch with the Shumways by an organization for families of M.I.A.'s."

Stone had brought back the son of Mr. and Mrs. Shumway, now a man in his mid-thirties, who had spent the last decade of his life as an M.I.A./P.O.W. at a prison camp in northern Laos that Mark and his team had decimated before pulling out with Chris Shumway and three other P.O.W.'s, two Americans and an Australian. As usual, the operation had been concealed from all media and government authorities.

"Husband or brother?" asked Mark.

Nora Bradford handed him an envelope. Mark opened it and extracted a snapshot of a husky-looking man in U.S. Army fatigues, against a backdrop of green jungle hills and washed-out blue sky that Mark recognized as Vietnam.

"My husband, Alex," she said as Stone studied the picture. "That's the last known photograph of him. It's years old, of course. Alex was a pilot. He was lost over Laos in the last year of the war. He was listed as M.I.A. I thought . . . all of these years . . . I thought he was dead."

"Have you remarried?" asked Stone.

It was not an idle question. Mark had learned early in

his M.I.A. work that to understand the emotional backgrounds of the people with whom he became involved on these missions was often the most valuable element.

"I never fell in love . . . after Alex," said Mrs. Bradford. "I don't know why. No, I never remarried. I guess it's because I've always hoped and prayed deep in my heart that Alex was alive somewhere. That he'd be found . . . and brought home to me."

"What have you learned that makes you think your husband is alive?"

"This civilian M.I.A. organization I mentioned got in touch with me," she said. "They have ways of intercepting some government agency field reports regarding reported sightings of American P.O.W.'s in Indochina." With an expression of real pain and uncertainty, Nora Bradford halfway turned to face the man who sat beside her. "I don't understand, Mr. Stone. How can our government be aware of these sightings—there've been so many!—and not take some kind of action on the matter?"

"We're afraid to wield the power we hold," growled Mark. "This country hasn't lost its guts; we've just been turning the other cheek."

"Sylvia Shumway told me that you . . . help people with loved ones in those P.O.W. camps."

"You haven't told me why you think Alex is still alive," he reminded her.

"I've received word through the M.I.A. organization that a group of anti-Communist Free Lao guerrillas encountered an American P.O.W. in the Xieng Khouang province of Laos. The circumstances aren't clear. The report was very sketchy. The American had escaped from a P.O.W. camp in the mountains. He apparently encountered the guerrillas just as troops from the camp, Viet soldiers, caught up with him.

"Most of the guerrillas were killed in an exchange with

the troops. Only one of the Free Lao fighters escaped. It was another ten days or so before he could pass on the account to a C.I.A. contact in Vientiane. The guerrilla only knew the American's last name—Bradford.

"That is good enough for me, Mr. Stone. I'm willing to bet that my husband is alive. I want to do everything in my power to see that Alex is brought home before his suffering grows even worse."

Mark could appreciate that, perhaps more than Nora Bradford would ever know. Mark's last stop in Vietnam before the end of the war had been a North Viet P.O.W. camp, where he had been imprisoned in a living nightmare that would haunt him forever.

Stone's captivity had been listed on "official records" by Hanoi, and he was released after the signing of treaties in a widely publicized media event orchestrated to show the humanitarianism of the North Vietnamese.

When Stone got back to the States, he was offered a commission. But he turned it down. He was disillusioned with an army and a government that would not commit action to rescuing those of his comrades who had fought for that army and government, yet were still being held prisoner in Southeast Asia long after an unpopular war that no one wanted to remember.

Mark made no profit whatever from his M.I.A.-hunting operations. His fees covered only expenses and personnel. Stone's motivation arose from his intimate knowledge of what it was like to starve in a bamboo cage in 105-degree heat, to be tortured by a barbaric camp commandant or sadistic guards.

Mark could not shake the nagging feeling of guilt that gnawed at his soul ever since he had been paraded in front of cameras as a freed P.O.W., knowing that other, unaccounted-for American prisoners were still being detained by the Viets.

"Your intel is good enough for me, too," he told Nora Bradford. "I took the liberty of tracing your name and verifying your story before we met."

"Then you know that I have money," she told him. "I can afford whatever expenses you incur."

"You'll be billed if and when I return with your husband, or proof of what happened to him," said Mark. "I've already sent for the men who will accompany me on this mission. We'll be flying out tomorrow."

When he began his career as an M.I.A. hunter, Stone had been realistic enough to know he could never tackle such work alone. He was already well connected in the international community of soldiers of fortune, and had at his disposal a roster of twenty-seven men with whom he'd served at one time or another in 'Nam—men he trusted, with whom he had maintained casual friendships right up until the present. Mark called this roster his Green List, a network of mercs handpicked to assure that no opportunistic, trigger-happy hotshots would accompany him into battle.

Stone's team were not men out to make a quick buck, but men who shared his background and opinions, who knew exactly what they were doing in life and in combat, which are often the same thing. Stone's allies in these M.I.A. missions were assisting him in the rescue of P.O.W.'s for their own personal reasons.

Mark only hired men who cared. Men like Terrance Loughlin and Hog Wiley, whom he had sent for a day ago, after having verified who Nora Bradford was and that in all likelihood he would accept the assignment she offered him.

He realized that Mrs. Bradford was studying him intently in the moonlight that filtered into the car. It was not a romantic appraisal, but more as if the lady were trying somehow to better understand this man, the likes of whom she had probably not encountered since beginning her recent odyssey through bureaucratic red tape and no-can-do.

"You're offering to go over to that godforsaken country and risk your life for a man you never met, and you're not worried about being paid for it. What makes you tick, Mr. Stone?"

"I don't really think about it." Stone was already getting out of her vehicle when he added, "I'll just try my best to bring your husband home, Mrs. Bradford."

Chapter Three

Stone spent much of the long flight trying to sleep, to store away energy for the rigors he knew were ahead for him and his men. After they landed in Bangkok, there was no telling when the next slowdown point would come.

Stone wanted to be rested for the total immersion in a foreign culture that would occur when he and his men stepped off their flight.

When time for sleep did come, it would be under tense, taut-nerved conditions where anything more than a one-eyed catnap could get you killed. The waking hours in the oppressive mugginess would dull the senses and, combined with lack of sleep, could also be fatal.

A man had to be in top physical shape, the way Stone and his men were, even to begin, much less survive, the strenuous path through hell that he knew lay ahead.

But deep sleep was elusive, and what he experienced was a fitful on-again-off-again half-sleep, deep enough only for dreams fueled by conscious memory.

There are few things a man can experience that will stick with him like the impressions of war gained first-hand. Stone considered his memories of his days as a P.O.W. to be the prime motivator of his life and M.I.A. work. Memories of that living nightmare tremored through his conscious thoughts at least once a day; they were seared into his soul.

On the flight to Bangkok, Stone dreamed. His dreams were of those days...

Mark had been with Special Forces in a fortified jungle hamlet. The hamlet had been low on the U.S. command's priority list, but all that changed in the closing days of the war. By the time Stone got there, it was too damn late, but he did his best, which in this case had proved to be not enough.

The night the dozens of N.V.A. regulars came blazing out of the jungle treeline was a night of massacre that Mark had been unable to avert. He blazed away with his M-16, joining the militiamen who stayed to fight.

Death was all around them that night. Stone saw the enemy stumble and fall beneath the steady hammering of his M-16, and he saw the Cong open fire on women and children in the village who tried to scurry to safety, as well as on the militiamen who were overrun by the first wave of the attack.

A concussion grenade blew Mark out from his cover behind some lumber and tossed him into unconsciousness amid the sounds of battle and the screams of the slaughtered fading into a chilled black hole of nothing...

When he came to, Stone knew immediately that they must have transported him across the border into Cambodia. The terrain was forest instead of jungle.

He awoke to pain hammering between his temples and

sweat stinging his eyes, glazing his vision, the buzzing of flies everywhere, and shrill, almost womanlike shrieks of pain from someone very close by.

Stone tried to move, and realized that he was chained to a coarse brick wall—chained with arms and legs outstretched, tugging uncomfortably.

The screams were those of a Vietnamese, also chained up, being interrogated and slowly castrated by men who paid no attention to Mark Stone.

Another squad of N.V.A. marched into the dank dungeon that smelled of feces and blood. They unshackled Stone and nudged him along with their AK-47s past the now unconscious man shackled to the wall, whose "interrogators" were attempting to revive the wretch so the "questioning" could continue.

The stench and the flies were worse outside. The prisoner-of-war camp was a loose circle of concrete blockhouses painted a muddy green to blend in with the foliage.

Stone saw a five-deep pile of dead, stripped human bodies stacked like cordwood behind the building he had just been taken from. The dead all looked Asian, most probably Vietnamese, and the victim who had been shackled alongside Mark would be stacked atop that pile as soon as he died. They were "interrogating" these poor devils to get a better stranglehold on South Vietnam's many anti-Communist factions.

A captured American was a different story.

Stone was led into a stuffy, bare, windowless office occupied by a desk and an N.V.A. officer, who did not stand but coolly observed as the four regulars herded Stone to a stop so that he faced the officer.

"I am Lieutenant Trang," the officer snapped in French-accented English. "What unit are you with, soldier?"

Stone gave his name, rank, and serial number.

"That will not do," Trang snapped. "You have seen what goes on here. Not pleasant, but necessary. And considerably more unpleasant for you than for us. We have a letter you will sign."

"Stuff your letter," Stone snarled, "where the sun don't shine. You won't kill me, Trang. You think you've got too many uses for me, but you won't get even one. You won't kill me either, because a captured American is always good to negotiate with."

"Perhaps we will not kill you," Trang conceded. "But I think we can make existence here unbearable enough for you that you will see things our way." Trang glanced at his soldiers. "Take him. I want the letter signed."

Stone's "interrogators" were human animals who specialized in torture. They used matches on him. They strung him up and beat him. One of them was expert in the use of metal bars and straps, skilled at twisting a man into all sorts of distorted positions to induce pain, knowing just how far to bend arms and legs without breaking limbs.

Stone did not sign the letter.

More prisoners continued to arrive during the time Mark was held there—more Vietnamese men and women, for "interrogation" in the Cambodian death camp that could have sprung from a Dante nightmare, except that nothing this hellish could be truly imagined without the real horror of having experienced it. Stone thought at one point that he could wish this on no man...except those who now held him prisoner along with the handful of other American P.O.W.'s.

These men Stone came to know. Wilcox. Mandrell. A few others were too near death to communicate through the bars of the cells in which they were imprisoned.

There was not enough room in a cell to stand with arms extended, not enough space to sleep stretched out. No toilet, no bed. Just the flies and the nerve-scraping screams from the building next door.

The hardest part in this hellhole, though, the four of them had agreed, even worse than the physical punishment, was the sense of being so completely cut off from civilization. The world these men came from could have been another planet, they were so isolated here in the Cambodian frontier. The isolation could warp the soul and twist the mind, and the *ultimate* fear—even worse than dying, because death was all around and you became numb even to that—the *real* fear was that you had been forgotten by the very ones you had fought for, that they wanted nothing to do with you, now that fate had tossed you a bum roll of the dice.

The fear of being forgotten, of being as adrift in this alien world as an astronaut cut adrift in deep space, was what drove one guy to the point of committing suicide by smashing his head repeatedly into the stone wall of his cell until he died.

Those prisoners strong enough to walk or talk, including Mark, were taken from their cells several times a month to be further "interrogated." Schweiker died of a heart attack when they went to work on him with the metal bars and straps one day. Newton, Stevens, and Stone were soon the only American P.O.W.'s left, and each of them had been pushed almost too many times to the edge of endurance. But the fight never left them. They were American servicemen sworn not to cooperate with their captors and to attempt every means of escape possible. The only trouble was, no means of escape ever appeared. There were no exercise periods, nothing like that. There was life in the cell, and meals of cold rice and water, and the only time the Americans were taken from their cells was under heavy guard for further "questioning" by the sadistic Trang, who always made a point of being present when there was torture to be done.

The American P.O.W.'s did get their chance, though, thanks to Mark Stone.

It happened late one night when most of the camp was asleep.

Except for Lieutenant Trang.

Trang was awake—blind drunk but awake—and the sadistic streak in the bastard flared to the surface. The camp officer strutted into the stinking cell block right past the sentry. Trang stood outside the row of cells of Stevens, Newton, and Stone. Trang woke them from their fitful slumber, railed at them in his native tongue, spat at them, called them names they could not understand though the general idea came across clearly enough.

Then the taunting drunk made a mistake and came too close to Stone's cell, and suddenly, in a blinding moment of clarity, nothing mattered to Stone except stretching his hands out lightning-fast between the bars of his cell. His hands clasped around Trang's throat and he pulled and twisted brutally, sharply. The officer had time only to gurgle out a gasp of surprise. His eyes popped, then Stone snapped his neck and Trang's face turned purple and he stopped gasping, his tongue out of his mouth like a rotting sausage and his knees buckling. The dead officer collapsed sideways to lie an equal distance from each of the three cells.

The body of Trang was found in the morning, and then the *real* interrogation almost began—except for the word that spread like wildfire throughout the camp that same morning Trang's body was found.

The war was over.

As abruptly as that, it did not seem to matter anymore which of the three American prisoners had slain the officer.

Stone and his buddies were shipped out that same day to be used as human poker chips, with which the powers that be could negotiate compromise and concession.

* * *

The hell of that prison compound had never left Mark Stone's conscious or subconscious mind. The driving wheel, clearer, more painful than ever, priming Stone for action, aboard a present-day flight to Bangkok...

Chapter Four

"I don't believe this frigging rush hour."

Hog Wiley pushed the rental car along a Bangkok street that seemed to be awash in traffic, packed from curb to curb with every conceivable mode of transportation known to man. Cars like theirs were in the clear minority. Most of the traffic was made up, it seemed, of jostling pedestrians, motorcycles, and bicycles—some of them attached to carts and made to serve as rickshaws.

The crowded street was typical, and it was always rush hour in the capital city of Thailand. Five million people lived inside the city limits—ten percent of the little jungle nation's population crowded into one place, struggling for the right to make a living, seeking room to breathe.

The human stew of faces, Oriental faces with a sprinkling of Anglos, reminded Mark Stone of Saigon before the Fall, before it was rechristened Ho Chi Minh City. The scenes were similar, as every major city of the East was similar, but they were not identical. In Bangkok there was nothing of the military presence that had been so omnipresent in Saigon at war. The uniforms were there, all right, if you took time to look for them, but they did not intrude upon and dominate the scene.

The capital had become almost a Western outpost in a sea of creeping red. The agents of a dozen different governments convened here, sharp ears tuned and listening to eastward for the slightest hint of new intelligence from inside the hostile camp. And as for the Communists, they had their agents handy too, prepared to pass out their disinformation on demand, to sabotage and even murder in pursuit of leaks that threatened their security.

Any agent who had ever done a tour in Berlin would recognize Bangkok without a second glance. The atmosphere of danger and intrigue, a heady incense of deceit and peril, hung above the city like a pall. It could reach out and suffocate the uninitiated, the unwary—or it could provide a seasoned warrior with the scent he needed to pursue his cause.

Hog knew the town well enough to locate the riverfront district without directions from Stone, and within twenty minutes they were cruising slowly on the long streets.

The three of them were on their way to keep a date with one An Khom, a dealer in the instruments of war. He was not listed in the telephone directories, or registered with any local chamber of commerce, but in his way the weapons specialist was every bit as famous in the Asian underworld as John D. Rockefeller had been in old New York. He was the top of the line, the best, and he could do the impossible—for a price.

Their meetings in the past had been infrequent, brief, but Stone had trusted old An Khom enough to place the order with him for the hardware they would need this time. If nothing else, he knew the old man could produce the needed weapons, and keep his mouth shut about it in the process.

For the moment, it was all Stone needed.

They had timed the rendezvous for sundown, when the pickup would be covered by descending darkness, and now the time was drawing near. Stone checked his watch and flicked a glance at Hog, behind the wheel, silently willing the huge Texan to milk some more speed out of the car, to get them through the throngs of people and on to their destination on time.

Hog was glaring at the rearview mirror, chewing over something that he didn't like the taste of. It took another moment for him to confirm, and underneath the beard, his rugged face was set into an angry mask as he began to speak.

"Aw, shit. We've got a tail."

The others did not turn around to check their backtrail. No point in tipping off the opposition that their presence had been noted.

"Are you sure?" Loughlin asked unnecessarily.

"Sure, I'm sure. The last two turns were just for them. They're hanging tight."

"Well, dammit."

Stone was thinking fast, calculating probabilities, and he was ready for an answer when Hog spoke again.

"You want I should shake 'em?"

"Negative," he snapped. "Until we know the players, let's not make any sudden moves."

"You figure C.I.A.?"

Mark shrugged resignedly.

"Who knows? Could be anybody."

And that was the hell of it. In Thailand, here and now, the secret operatives of half a hundred nations were at work, gathering intelligence about Vietnamese, Laotians, Cambodians, Chinese. Bangkok and points east served the same listening-post function for the West in Asia that Berlin served in Europe, or Hong Kong along the Chinese mainland.

Not that it was free of Communists—far from it. China, Vietnam, the Soviets...all had their men and women in Bangkok, their ears to the underground, picking up whatever fell unguarded through the fine net of security. It was a two-way street, and it was every bit as crowded as the city's other, more apparent avenues of commerce.

"Take them to the drop," Stone said at last, not missing the sudden startled glance he got from Hog.

"You sure about that?"

"I'm sure. We can't afford to miss this pickup, and the dealer can look out for himself. He's been at it long enough."

Law of the jungle, damned right, and they were in the jungle now. It didn't take a sea of trees and liana vines to hide the predators who stalked them in Bangkok, and they would have to be every bit as cautious in the city as they would out in the bush.

As for An Kohm, he was a born survivor. Stone was not concerned about the possibility of leading their pursuers to his door. The old man had not come so far, survived so long in his chosen field, by allowing himself to be vulnerable.

"We're almost there."

Hog managed a slow, awkward lane change, drifting toward the left-hand curb and setting himself up for the turn. Their new street was narrower than the last, and if anything, it seemed more congested with jostling humanity. Wiley restrained himself from leaning on the horn, but it was taking all the self-control he had to keep from rolling down a window and telling all these jostling crowds to get the hell out of his way, and fast.

"Up there, right side. The pagoda front."

"Gotcha."

"See if you can work your way around into the alley at the rear."

"Will do."

It took nearly ten minutes to cover the last half-block and turn into a narrow alley just beyond their target, but they finally made it, picking up some angry glares from gesturing pedestrians and bicyclists along the way. Hog returned them all with equanimity, his lifted middle finger offering the old salute to all and sundry.

As they rumbled down the alley, crunching trash beneath their tires, Stone risked a backward glance and saw their tail slide by in traffic. Black and squarish, it was a typical government car, but which government? The face that turned to glance at him, and just as swiftly turned away, was white. It might have been American or British, even Russian.

Never mind. He put the riddle into storage for the moment, concentrating on the task at hand. They had arrived, and nothing must prevent them from securing the supplies he had ordered from An Khom. Nothing. Anyone who got in their way from this point on was asking for trouble of the terminal variety.

Stone hoped it wasn't C.I.A., but in the last analysis, it really didn't matter. His own government had written off the M.I.A's, from all appearances, aligned themselves with all the other groups and nations who were too complacent, too goddamned self-satisfied about the end of the war to care whether several thousand innocents remained behind to pay the price in perpetuity. And while Stone would not have considered shooting down a government employee under any circumstances in the States, it was a different ballgame in the Asian jungle killing grounds.

Out here, all men were equal, and all whites were aliens, intruders. The C.I.A. had license to pursue its interests here, of course, but that was license out of Washington, and it was no more binding on Mark Stone than was the warrant issued on him out of Ho Chi Minh City some months earlier.

He would cooperate with anyone who helped him—and God help the bastards who opposed him in his efforts to release the long-suffering prisoners he sought.

Hog found a parking place, or made his own, and killed the engine. In the alley, dusk had become darkness.

"Want me to stick with the car?" Wiley asked.

"Yeah. We'll check inside, and call you when it's time to shift the load."

"Roger that."

Stone and Loughlin left the rental car and crossed the narrow alley, working their way up a side street to the avenue they had only lately left. They would have to approach the pagoda from the front, its only public entrance, and they risked exposure in the process, but they had no choice. If there was trouble waiting for them, they would find it—or it would find them—soon enough.

Chapter Five

From dusk, they entered into stygian darkness. It required a moment for their eyes to adjust to the light of distant candles, flickering in the gloom around a smallish altar at the far end of the room.

The air was thick with incense, almost choking, and the smell of it brought back a flood of memories for Stone. Another tour of duty, in another time and place, with other enemies.

No, scratch that. He was still up against the same damned enemy. The same eternal enemy. The names had changed, and the faces, but the evil that they worked was still the same, unaltered.

And if the war required his presence in a temple, he could live with it, although he had no firm belief in any higher power, any guiding hand.

They paced off the pagoda's central aisle, moving toward the altar, cautious in the semidarkness of the unfamiliar room. They were alone, or so it seemed, but warriors never trust luck or take security for granted.

Stone kept one hand inside the jacket he wore despite the heat, and under there, his fingers rested on the butt of his Beretta 93-R. Smuggling it aboard aircraft was becoming more and more of a challenge, especially with the renewed spate of hijackings stateside, but he managed, with a little ingenuity. And it was comforting to touch the cool steel now; it seemed to drive the shadows back and hold them at bay.

Beside the altar was an open doorway, screened with long strings of hanging plastic beads. Stone led the way, brushing through the rustling curtain, Loughlin close upon his heels.

They found themselves inside an empty anteroom with doors on either side. Stone searched his memory, trying to recall whether it was to the right or the left, finally deciding on the latter. He was reaching out to knock, his right hand still occupied beneath the jacket, when a voice behind them startled him.

"Welcome to Bangkok," it said.

The warriors spun around, and the Beretta was no longer sheathed as Stone prepared to face the enemy. Instead, he found himself the object of scrutiny for two narrow, dark, familiar eyes.

It was An Khom.

There was no door behind the tiny figure, at least none that Stone or Loughlin could detect, but they refrained from asking how the little Oriental had moved up behind them with such stealth. Stone knew that if he had the time and the need, he could search out the secret passageway behind the altar.

For the moment it was not required, and so he let it go, dismissed the puzzle from his thoughts. He sheathed his weapon, bowing slightly from the waist in greeting.

"An Khom."

"Welcome," the old man repeated. "I have been expecting you for some time."

Stone and Loughlin exchanged cautious glances.

"We picked up an unexpected tail," Stone told him simply.

A flicker of what might have been concern was visible upon the timeless face, then quickly vanished.

"They traced you here? No matter. What is meant to come will come."

An Khom turned away and led them through a doorway—to the left, as Stone had remembered. Once beyond it, they were in a sort of mini-warehouse that abutted on the alley where their car was parked with Hog on guard.

A glance around the place did not reveal their shipment, but Stone waited, biding his time until the old man found a seat behind the desk that seemed to be the only furniture.

"You have the things I ordered?" he inquired at last.

"Of course. CAR-15 assault carbines. One thousand rounds of ammunition each, in magazines. The various grenades: concussion, thermite, fragmentation."

"What about the plastic?" Loughlin asked. He was the powder man, the team's explosives expert, and he never liked to travel far without the tools of his trade at hand.

An Khom seemed amused by the Britisher's impatience.

"Certainly," he answered. "As ordered. Fifty pounds of C-4, strictly military grade. I also have the timers, fuses, detonators—everything you need."

"I'm counting on it," Stone informed him, and the soldier's tone made it clear that everything had better be secure, in working order, on delivery.

"As for the matter of my payment—"

Stone thrust a hand into the inside pocket of his coat, withdrew a wad of bills, and started peeling off the large ones, counting silently. He handed them across, and watched as An Khom started riffling through them, doing a fast count of his own. "Fifty thousand bahts, as agreed," Stone told him, knowing that the little gnome would count it anyway.

It was a little over two thousand dollars, American, and Stone counted himself fortunate at that. Some dealers in the area might have asked twice as much for the shipment he required, but prior dealings with An Khom had taught the soldier how to bargain with him, talk him down until the margin of profit was reduced to a manageable two or three hundred percent.

The Asian finished his count and pocketed the money with a narrow smile, devoid of warmth.

"Perfect. A glass of wine to consummate the bargain?"

Stone shook his head. It was his turn to be impatient now.

"No time." He glanced around the obviously empty room. "You have the shipment here?"

An Khom shook his head, a curt negative.

"This is my business office, nothing more. As you have amply demonstrated, it is not secure."

"Where, then?"

"I will take you there, but first it will be necessary for you to divest yourself of shadows."

Loughlin looked confused.

"What's that?"

"We've got to clip the tail," Stone translated for him.

The Britisher smiled.

Stone knew the look, the eagerness for combat, and he frowned.

"Nothing permanent, unless they force it."

Now Loughlin looked a fraction disappointed.

"Very well. I'll only ding them up a little."

"Right."

"When you are finished, we can start," the Asian said, helping himself to a glass of the amber wine without rising from behind his desk.

And so they had to clip the tail. All right. But first they

had to find the men who were pursuing them. If the trackers had been sticking close, there was no problem. But if they had broken off upon identifying their location, it might be impossible to trace them now.

Either way, they had to make the effort, clean their skirts before they asked the Asian weapons dealer to reveal his hiding place.

Stone and his companion left the office, doubling back along their tracks. There was no need for conversation, and they moved along in silence toward the beaded curtain, which rustled like an artificial waterfall.

And Stone was instantly alert to danger.

Several moments had elapsed since they met An Khom. Time enough, and more, for the strings of beads to come to rest, stop jostling one another. They were moving now, and that could only mean that they had been disturbed.

A draft, perhaps—or else a human hand, pushing back the strands to take a look inside.

Stone was counting on the latter option as he eased the black Beretta from its armpit holster, slipped the safety lever off and into firing mode. Beside him, Loughlin tensed but made no move to draw a weapon of his own.

They slipped through the curtain one at a time, merging with the partial darkness of the temple room. They crouched beside the altar, sheltered from the candles by a little overhang, trying not to breathe the stifling incense smoke any more than was absolutely necessary.

"Company?" the Britisher whispered, his voice almost inaudible though inches from Stone's ear.

Stone shrugged, scarcely moving with the gesture, and his eyes were raking the rows of wooden benches, seeking any kind of movement that might give away the presence of an enemy.

One minute, two . . . and he was sweating, from the musty heat inside the room and from the tension mounting up inside him. He could feel the old battle-eagerness himself, now, in the tingling of his spine, the sudden tightness of his testicles, and he was ready.

Ready to fight.

Ready to kill, if it came to that.

Another moment, and he had his target. Dark, and barely visible above the back of a bench three rows from the rear.

A human shape was rising from a crouch, inching along the row and toward the center aisle. From there, it would be twenty feet to freedom and the street—if he could make it.

"There?"

Stone pointed, hissing out the warning, but Loughlin already had the opposition spotted in the semidarkness. He was moving now, swift and catlike on the balls of his feet, edging away from the altar.

When he made the break, he moved like lightning, and the opposition never really had a chance to see him coming. Downrange, the figure had risen to a stooping crouch, gaining the aisle, already swiveling toward the inviting safety of the exit. Loughlin covered the thirty feet in seconds flat, launching himself into a flying tackle when he was but halfway to the human target.

And he scored, his shoulder driving hard against the small of the creeper's back, punching the wind out of him as it drove him to the floor with a startled little cry.

At once, a second figure vaulted up and out of the pew behind his comrade and the Britisher, pivoting to bring a weapon up and onto target. He was aiming straight at Loughlin, lining up the shot, and he would put a bullet through the warrior's bobbing skull, unless—

On an impulse, Stone restrained the killer urge without sacrificing speed or accuracy. The black Beretta was already climbing, swinging onto target by the time he recognized his good friend's danger, and the last adjustment took only a heartbeat to realize.

He stroked the trigger once, again, and two hot Parabellum stingers closed the gap, slamming into the wooden pew mere inches from his human target. They exploded into shards of wood and copper jacketing, a sudden storm directly in the hostile gunner's face, which spoiled his aim and sent his own revolver bullet whining into empty darkness.

The opposition wasn't waiting for a second chance. With a survivor's instinct, he abandoned his companion to whatever fate awaited him and vaulted up and away from there, hurdling the bench and diving for the doorway on his own. He fanned a backward shot in Stone's direction, but his haste and lack of time to aim deprived him of a killing shot. A foot to Stone's left, a candleholder toppled, spinning from the bullet's impact.

Stone was after him before the gunshot's echoes died away inside the temple. Sprinting down the aisle, he leaped across the struggling forms of Loughlin and his captive, heard the panting, cursing voices mingled into one as the men grappled in the darkness.

There was nothing he could do at present; Loughlin would secure his man, or lose him—but the second tail was definitely freedom-bound unless Stone could overtake him on the street and bring him down.

It would be touchy, seeking out a faceless stranger in the city, trying to secure him without attracting the attention of police—but Stone would have to try.

He gained the sidewalk just in time to see his adversary disappearing down the alley they had used to reach the main pagoda entrance. The race was still ahead of him, and he could not begin to see the finish line from where he stood.

Mark Stone put everything he had into that race, pounding off the yards of pavement like a young Olympic aspirant, aware that everything was riding on the outcome of his run. If he should miss his chance, allow the tail to slip away, would An Khom exercise his rights and refuse to make delivery? If delivery was even delayed, their plan was jeopardized, perhaps fatally. Time was of the essence now to all concerned, and if the dominoes were falling prematurely, it could be the end for all of them.

Most especially for Colonel Alex Bradford.

If he was alive.

Stone meant to find the answer for himself, and that meant taking one step at a time. *This* step, right now.

He was a dozen yards behind the other runner when they reached the second turn—and then, incredibly, Stone's quarry was turning *left,* in the direction of their car, and the soldier felt a sudden surge of hope.

Hog Wiley was there, and he was on his station. When the runner made the corner, pounding down the alley, Hog became curious. When Stone appeared in hot pursuit, the curiosity gave way to action, and the bearded giant moved with speed and grace deceptive for a person of his size. He was out of the car, vaulting across the still-warm hood and taking up his place across the runner's path before a conscious plan had time to form.

The runner saw him, but too late. He tried to veer around the obstacle, but Hog's long arm was reaching out, the fingers tangling in his suit lapel and hauling him up, almost off his feet. A fist the size of a Christmas ham was rushing at his face with freight-train speed, and there was only time for him to give a strangled cry before the crushing impact.

Stone broke his stride, trotting toward the car where Hog now had their captive draped across the hood like some bizarre hunting trophy.

"This one almost got away," the big man jibed.

"Like hell. I have to give you one from time to time," Mark answered with a trace of a smile.

Chapter Six

Loughlin found the empty black sedan a block down, to the east, and keys secured from the pocket of one opposition agent let them bring it on around in back of the pagoda. Another moment saw both silent figures loaded in the trunk and locked there, momentarily secure from prying eyes.

The problem now was what to do with them.

Mark Stone had no intention now of killing them, not after all the trouble he had gone through just to capture them alive. At the same time, they could not be allowed to communicate with their headquarters until Stone and his companions were away and running free toward their destination and the arms they had come to pick up from An Khom. In the end it was decided that the trackers would remain exactly where they were, and that their car would be abandoned in a public place, where someone would be sure to hear their cries for help and let them out—within a day or two, at any rate.

Hog was chuckling as he rested on the trunk lid, one leg

cocked across the other.

"Somebody's gonna be a little limp before they get out of that sweatbox."

And from Hog's tone of voice, it was clear that he did not mind the thought at all.

"Their problem," Stone replied. "Come on, we've got a pickup to make."

He tossed the second pair of keys to Hog, and motioned to him to climb behind the wheel of the enemy tail car.

"Follow us until I give the signal, then we'll wait while you drop off the package and regroup."

"Roger that."

The big man climbed into the driver's seat, filling it with his sizable bulk. He waited there as Stone went back inside the temple to collect the British soldier and their guide, An Khom.

"You'll ride with us," he told the little Oriental. "No point taking three cars on a simple run like this."

"My pleasure."

There was something like a glint of humor there, behind the old man's eyes, and Stone knew he was seeing through the small talk and the crap, picking up on the real motive for Stone's order. Too much had gone wrong already on a simple mission, and Stone was not taking any further chances with their guide. He had already paid up front, and there was no way in the world An Khom would get out of his sight until the arms were safely in possession of his team.

They waited while the old man locked the entrance to his temple-cum-business office, and the tall men flanked him on their short walk to the waiting car. He looked like a wrinkled, malnourished child between them, but his bearing had the dignity of years behind it, and his face was filled with hard-won wisdom that no child could ever bear. As they walked together, Stone found himself briefly wondering about the old man, probing at him with a dozen silent questions that he knew would never be asked aloud. What made a man like this, of obvious social rank and breeding, turn to trading in the toys of death? What kept him here, in what might any day become a powder keg, when he could clearly find the cash to settle anywhere he liked?

No matter. An Khom's reasons were his own, and none of Stone's concern. A man had choices from the cradle to the grave, and he would answer for his own selections in his own good time. As for Mark Stone, he had made choices of his own along the way, which just might get him killed unless the old arms dealer had their weaponry on hand and in good working order.

They reached the rental car and scrambled in, all three of them together in the broad front seat, with An Khom in the middle. Loughlin took the wheel, and Stone rode shotgun, with his jacket open and the sleek Beretta easily available.

"All right," he told their passenger. "Your show."

An Khom supplied them with enough directions to get started in an easterly direction, and from prior visits to Bangkok, Stone recognized their course as leading in the general direction of the wealthy, hilly suburbs laid out in a horseshoe pattern halfway around the teeming city. The arms, of course, could be stashed anywhere between their starting point and the city limits, but a nagging hunch was growing in the soldier's mind, and he decided to check it out.

"Where's the stash?" he asked offhandedly, his tone conveying nothing more than casual interest.

"Excuse me, please?"

"The merchandise. Where is it?"

"Safe. I keep the major shipments at my home, outside the city proper."

Loughlin cast a sidelong glance at An Khom, the surprise apparent on his face.

"The weapons are inside your home?"

The Oriental flashed a cagy smile, including both men in its scope.

"Where else could they be more secure? The competition in my business is . . . intense. Some of my competitors are ruthless, verging on the common criminal. I buy a certain amount of official protection, of course, but still . . ."

They were passing out of the downtown area now, and entering the slums that somehow always seem to flower in the shadow of a thriving business district. Houses in name only slumped together, row upon reeking row of clapboard, tin, and tarpaper fashioned into dwellings that might house a single family or three or more in putrid squalor. Garbage lined the streets and overflowed the large communal dumpsters that were situated at the corners in a feeble gesture toward some now-forgotten effort to clean up the city. Each dumpster had its little clique of scavengers picking through the rubbish, scrounging for their evening meal. Around their feet, the ubiquitous scrawny dogs were waiting for the scraps their masters missed, and running constant risk of being added to the cooking pot themselves.

Every man becomes a child again when he enters the slums of an Oriental city. There is nothing in the West, in Detroit or Newark or Buenos Aires, to compare with Asia's urban wastelands. Nowhere in the West—perhaps nowhere outside of Africa, and seldom there—could such a scene of human misery be tolerated as the natural order of things. No one seemed to question that these dwellers in the depths belonged exactly where they were, and Stone observed that An Khom did not seem to see them, could not seem to focus on their plight as children and old women flocked around the car, their hands outstretched and begging for some meager charity.

Loughlin cursed beneath his breath, but kept the car in motion for another several blocks until they lost the crowd. Stone cast a backward glance, making sure Hog was with them, hanging close. They traveled on another block, then two and three more, before Stone spied a dropoff point that satisfied him, on a lonely little side street.

At a word, their British driver nosed the car over and kept the engine running as Stone got out and walked back toward the approaching car with Hog at the wheel. He pointed out the drop, and was already moving back in the direction of his own car by the time Hog found a parking place beside the vacant lot.

Come sunup, this lot would be teeming with the hungry, homeless, jobless, urban refugees of wars gone by or still in progress. They would strip the car, of course, as soon as they determined there was no one near enough to stop them, and in the process they would free the captives from their metal prison. That would raise some eyebrows, set some feet in motion, right enough.

Stone almost wished that he could stay around and watch, but he had business elsewhere and it wouldn't keep.

When they were all together in the rental car, with Hog filling up the back seat with his girth, they set out once again.

"All right," Stone told their front-seat passenger. "We need an address. Now."

The old man simply smiled and nodded, rattling off directions to a street that Stone remembered as a pleasant, palm-lined circle dotted with beautiful homes. Not the most luxurious neighborhood in town, but getting there, and just the address gave him a close indication of the old man's net financial worth. Stone looked at him again, with new respect.

"You run a risk, An Khom. Your neighbors might not care for having arms and ammunition hidden so nearby."

The old Oriental shrugged, and once again the little, canny smile was back in place.

"How do you say it? 'What they don't know won't hurt me'?"

"Close enough," Stone answered, and he couldn't quite help grinning.

The old man was a savvy soldier, all right, and cool as ice, considering the hellfire business he was in. He was a valuable ally and associate, but he would make a ruthless enemy if it ever came to that.

Stone hoped it never would.

They were close to their destination and following An Khom's last-minute guidance when the sharp, pervasive odor of smoke hit them. The windows of the car were down, and it was coming from outside, somewhere ahead of them. And close by, from the smell of it.

"Somebody throwin' a barbecue around here?" Hog inquired, half-seriously.

In the seat beside Mark Stone, the old man was erect and suddenly alert. His tension was contagious, and the others sensed that they were moving into some potential danger, nameless yet, but all too real.

"What is it?" Stone asked, seeing An Khom's sudden agitation.

"Wait."

Just that, and nothing more. The old man was craning forward in his seat now, one hand on the dashboard, narrowed eyes probing at the night beyond the bright cones cut by their twin-beam headlights.

Another curve, and then the trees were clearing as a driveway opened up on their left. Behind a low retaining wall were more trees, and the suggestion of a large house in the middle distance. There were cars parked in the driveway, several of them, and a strange, dancing light illuminated figures running all along the drive, across the manicured lawn.

The house was burning, providing battlefield illumination for a scene straight out of hell.

And now, as if the silent curtain had been lifted, they could hear a crackle of distant gunfire, some of it confined, as if the shooters were inside the burning house. Out on the lawn, a pair of automatic weapons answered, spitting dirty yellow flame, gunners raking the façade of the house, pinning its occupants inside and keeping them from making their escape.

An Khom was trembling now, and Stone knew what was wrong with him as Loughlin hit the car's brakes, before the old man found his voice.

"That is my house!" the Asian groaned. "My family is inside!"

Chapter Seven

Stone was out of the car and moving on his own before it came to a halt, the black Beretta in his hand and ready. Loughlin and Hog Wiley hit the pavement a heartbeat later, each of them unlimbering the holstered hardware that he carried in concealment.

They had not come seeking battle, but the fight was theirs, for now. Perhaps within the burning house itself were weapons and explosives they had paid for in advance. If nothing else, they had a large investment to protect, including the success of their mission.

"Fan out and keep it low," Stone barked, aware that both of his soldiers already knew the routine. They had seen combat, and plenty of it, long before they joined his little band of manhunters. Each of them was able to protect himself in a killing situation, and to make long odds more comfortable than they had any right to be. Trained killers, yes, but killers in a cause. And neither man was here with Stone because he chose to sell his gun. Instead, they were committed to a cause, the oldest one around.

Good versus Evil, and the devil take the slackers.

Stone was moving out, his two men peeling off to either side, when An Khom passed him like a streak. He made a grab at the little darting figure, but his fingers only grazed the old man's jacket sleeve. In other circumstances he would not have thought An Khom had so much life left in him, but the weapons dealer saw his home and family going up in flames before his eyes, and he was definitely motivated now.

The soldier let him go, and old An Khom was lost within a moment, disappearing in the swirling smoke of battle. Of them all, he had the greatest right to be here, and Mark Stone did not have time or inclination now to try to hold him back.

There was enough for all of them to do, damned right, and Stone was in the thick of it from the moment he passed inside the arched gate of old An Khom's estate.

The grounds were spacious, and under other circumstances, in the sunshine, would have been a lovely vista. At the moment, with the backlighting of the flames and the pall of smoke hanging over everything, the landscape was more like a view of hell.

Three cars were parked along the curving driveway, carbon-copy limousines, each capable of carrying from eight to ten men. From where he stood in shadows, taking stock, Mark Stone could count perhaps a dozen running figures that he didn't recognize, approximately half of them equipped with automatic weapons. Most of them were occupied in firing at the house or running in its general direction, with a few men left behind to guard the cars.

He took advantage of the enemy's preoccupation to advance, but in his eagerness he almost met disaster. In the shadows to his right, a flanker with an automatic rifle saw his move and swiveled toward him, shouting a warning that was more surprise than anger.

In the end, it was the sentry's sudden noise that saved Stone's life. The guy could easily have dropped him cold if he had kept his wits about him, but the sudden shock of seeing an intruder had been too much for him. And that one mistake was all Stone needed.

Pivoting, he dropped to one knee, swinging his Beretta up and bracing it with both hands. A single stroke of the curving hair-trigger, and the pistol barked, the muzzle flash obscuring his target for an instant.

On the grim receiving end, his man was reeling, staggering away from there, a bloody hole where his left eye used to be. His dying brain, already mangled, sent a final signal to the hands, and his assault rifle ripped out an aimless burst into the night. It missed Stone by several yards, but it was more than loud enough to put his fellow gunners on alert.

Stone broke away from there, not waiting to see the lifeless target fall. He hit the fire-selector switch on his Beretta, setting it for automatic three-round bursts as he put ground between himself and the body of the sentry.

The shit was coming down, and he would need every ounce of firepower at his disposal to see his way through. At once, he put An Khom and all the others from his mind, instantly and totally preoccupied with his own survival.

Hog Wiley vaulted the chest-high wall with incredible grace and ease for a man of his size, landing in a fighting crouch on the other side. At once, the six-inch Colt Trooper .357 Magnum was in his giant fist, almost a live extension of himself as it swept the firelit darkness, seeking hostile targets.

He was on the hunt, and it felt good. Hog had been

missing combat since his last time out with Stone, and practice sessions at the range could only do so much to take the edge off, no matter how realistic they were made.

The fight was what he liked, what turned him on about his chosen martial trade, and here it was again, made to order. At the moment he didn't have the first idea who his enemies might be, and it didn't seem to matter in the least. Somewhere inside the house, his guns were burning up, if they were not already burned, and men with guns prevented him from saving them. It was enough for now.

He scanned the field, locating opposition soldiers by sound as much as by sight. He picked out the sounds of automatic weapons, and heard the flat, distinctive bark of Stone's Beretta when it joined the dance.

Hog moved, edging out and away from the wall in a crouch, keeping as low as possible, considering his bulk. Palm trees formed a marching line across the lawn, circling away to some point out behind the house, and he tried to keep them between himself and the crowd of running, dodging figures that were his eventual targets.

The longer he could keep his presence there a secret, the greater the surprise would be when he erupted in their midst, a shouting, shooting giant out of hell.

And sometimes, when he was outnumbered, the advantage of surprise could be enough to turn the tide. This time, perhaps.

He was twenty feet from the final line of palms when a shrieking figure burst from cover, charging directly at him on a collision course. Without thinking twice, Hog swung the Trooper up and squeezed the trigger, riding out the recoil of his doubly powerful hand-loaded cartridges, to watch the bullet impact on its rushing target.

It never failed to startle him, the way hot metal and soft flesh reacted at their meeting. When 158 grains of hollow-point thunder struck his target square upon the nose, a human face was suddenly wiped out, replaced by something sodden and no longer human, something flowing, in transition to another state of being. It became a liquid thing, and it could not command the body still appended to it. Limbs refused to answer signals from the newly hollowed skull, and as he watched, the running figure did a spastic little dance before collapsing into death.

There was no time to think about it now, for yet another figure was approaching on his left, this one closer, more determined. The second man was smart enough to squeeze the trigger of his weapon anyway, but he was too excited to make time for aiming, and the bullets whistled past an inch or two from Wiley's face.

The Texan dove into a flying shoulder roll, and came up several yards from where he had been standing. His adversary veered, attempting to regain his target, but he was too close for that, and it was much too late to compensate when Hog reached out to grasp his wrist in one giant, crushing hand. The little guy screamed and dropped his weapon as Hog twisted his arm, bringing it around in a swift arc until the bone snapped with a sound of dry twigs breaking underfoot. Hog shoved the smoking muzzle of his Colt into the screaming mouth and pressed the trigger, closing both his eyes against the sudden spray of blood and bone.

He let the headless dummy fall away from him and swiveled back to face the battle proper. Men were doubling back now, from the car and from the house, alerted by the sudden firing on their flank. Bullets were sweeping the darkness, seeking targets, most of them going wild but a few coming dangerously close. He found a palm and hugged it, his Trooper up and tracking, spitting death first at one target, then at another.

Hog was in his element, his glory. And with the possible exception of a certain whorehouse in L.A., he wouldn't have been elsewhere for the world.

• • •

Terrance Loughlin sighted through the drifting smoke and squeezed the trigger of his Browning Hi-Power auto-loading pistol. A single Parabellum slug went screaming into darkness, and the scream at once became a human one, already dwindling into liquid silence.

Unlike Hog, the Britisher did not love battle for its own sake. He had chosen a profession he was good at, for a multitude of reasons, and when he had been forced into premature retirement, he had marketed the only skills he possessed.

Not that Loughlin was a "simple" soldier, by any means. Behind the handsome face, the mind was active, alert, exceptional. But when confronted with the choice of turning mercenary or of sweating out his life behind a desk, in a flannel suit, there was—for him—no choice at all.

And maybe he was not so different from Hog, after all.

A gliding shadow in the darkness, Loughlin chose his targets carefully, selectively, attempting to fire only when the other guns were roaring, hoping to disguise his presence as long as possible. So far the enemy had not detected him— or else had not survived the brief and brutal meeting.

He was halfway to the house and closing fast when an explosion rocked the second story, flinging tiles and shingles skyward. Something very like a burning human form was catapulted from a second-story window, to land on the lawn and writhe there for several moments before death arrived to quench the flames.

He was about to call the house a write-off when the double doors in front burst open and a group of six or seven gunners hit the marble steps in a stampede. The Britisher could see a young woman struggling in their grasp as they beelined it for the waiting cars. An instant later, another little clutch of gunners came sprinting from the house, one pausing long enough to throw a burst of submachine-gun fire behind him through the doorway.

They were scattering, the nine or ten of them together with their hostage, fanning out among the waiting vehicles. Loughlin snapped his automatic up and sighted on the final straggler first, squeezing off a single round that picked him up and punched him around into a sloppy pirouette before it dropped him, lifeless, on the flagstone walkway.

They were at the cars, and piling in now, and he had no time to note which vehicle contained the woman. Never mind, the task was simple: to stop them—or as many of them as he could—from leaving the estate alive and with their hostage.

The lead car was rolling now, and veering in his general direction on the curving drive. Loughlin moved to meet it, his Browning up and ready in the classic duelist's stance, one arm outstretched, the other swung behind him to help balance him and hold him steady.

The car was about twenty yards away when the hostile driver saw and recognized his mortal danger. Loughlin put the Parabellum manglers out in rapid-fire, spent shell casings spinning, glinting in the firelight, tumbling through space.

A marching line of holes appeared across the car's windshield, milky spiderwebs of cracks now fanning out from each hole, obscuring the driver's view—which didn't matter anyhow, because the driver was dead behind the wheel, almost decapitated by the storm of lead and fractured glass that flayed him in his seat.

Without a hand upon the wheel, the car was turning, skidding, running straight at Loughlin as it jumped the curb and picked up speed. A dead foot held the pedal down, and the car was roaring now, caroming on across the lawn, on a collision course for the nearest row of palms.

Loughlin rolled aside and found his feet again in time to witness the collision. Irresistible force met immovable ob-

ject with a rending crash, and the palm tree was virtually
uprooted by the jarring impact. It teetered, rootless, for a
moment, then collapsed—directly on top of the auto that
had struck it.

The crushing weight of the tree crumpled steel and pinned
the screaming passengers inside. One of them was firing
wildly with a submachine gun, perhaps in fear or reflex
action, and an instant later his rounds found their target. A
spark flashed in the general location of the trunk, a bright
flame licking upward for a heartbeat just before it found the
fuel.

The detonation, when it came, was full of hollow thunder, rolling out across the lawn to flatten Loughlin where
he stood. The heat was searing, even at that range, and
there was not a hope in hell of anyone surviving in the heart
of it. A single scream erupted from the boxed inferno, and
was just as swiftly silenced by the hot, devouring flames.

Loughlin took himself away from there, his face a mask
of timeless fury as he tracked the other cars. It was high
time for him to chase the war.

Stone had seen the gunners leave the house with their
young female hostage, but he had a different vantage point
from Loughlin's. While the two surviving cars were pulling
off and leaving the Britisher behind them, they were actually
running straight for Stone, and he was determined to be
ready for them.

She was in the second remaining car, he knew that much,
and he had to stop the lead vehicle if he hoped to pen her
and her captors up inside the wall of old An Khom's estate.
For that, he would be needing something with more bite to
it than the Beretta had, and a heartbeat later Stone hit upon
the answer.

Several yards away, his latest kill was stretched across

the drive, an Uzi submachine gun inches from his lifeless hand. Stone made his move and plucked the weapon up perhaps a second or two after he saw the two surviving cars begin to roll his way.

And they were bearing down on him already, closing fast, the lead vehicle with three gunners in the front seat. Behind them in the other car, there would be two or three more, with the hostage that he hoped to free, but first he had to see about surviving on his own.

The Uzi was a favored weapon of guerrillas everywhere, light and compact, capable of spewing out the Parabellum man-breakers at a cyclic rate of 750 rounds per minute with a practiced finger on the trigger. Stone was practiced, but he had no way of knowing just how many rounds were left inside the captured weapon's magazine—and there was certainly no time to stop and look.

He put his trust in fate and held the trigger down, hosing the grill and windshield of the lead car as it barreled into his effective range. The deadly little slugs chewed through the grill and radiator, marching up across the hood and drilling through the safety glass to find flesh inside, and devour it.

His target started weaving at a range of fifty yards, and it was skidding broadside when the dying driver finally lost control completely. Stone saw it going over and into its death roll, and he knew that it would take him with it if he stood his ground much longer.

And he moved, departing from the line of fire perhaps a heartbeat before the rolling car thundered past. A door flopped open on the roll, disgorging a boneless body like so much discarded rubbish, and the car tumbled on, smoking now, with flames already licking the interior.

Behind it, the second driver saw his comrades die, and he reacted with exemplary control. A hard left twist, and

he was speeding up to put the ruined car between himself
and the anonymous machine gunner who so clearly meant
to kill them all. He gunned the accelerator, tires smoking,
chewing up grass and sod as he left the drive, running flat-
out and hell-for-leather right across the open lawn.

His gunner had the window down and was lining up an
AK-51 for the kill when Mark Stone saw it coming. A
sideways leap was all that saved him as the deadly steel-
jacketed rounds sliced air where he had stood but seconds
earlier.

And then the car was past him, roaring to the gate with
gunners and their hostage all intact, escaping. Stone came
up to one knee, the Uzi tracking, and he squeezed the trigger
and was instantly rewarded by a triple burst—and then
nothing. It was empty, slide locked open on the vacant,
smoking chamber. His three rounds cut the last car's rear
fender, flaking paint and gouging metal, then it was gone
and running free, already out of sight.

Stone dropped the useless Uzi and retrieved his pistol
from its shoulder harness. Silently he waited, listening to
the sound of tortured tires on pavement as the car escaped,
and hearing the closer crackling of the flames as they devoured the manor house behind him.

There was no more gunfire, no more shouting and
screaming. Alone with the dead, Mark Stone stood up and
went to find the living.

Chapter Eight

Stone should have known better.

This firefight at An Khom's wasn't over. Not yet. Not by a damn sight.

A heartbeat after the surviving limo had disappeared from Stone's sight into the gaping maw of darkness beyond the flickering illumination from An Khom's flaming house, Stone heard the roaring approach of another car. He turned to see the vehicle in which he and his company had arrived, with Hog Wiley at the wheel.

He saw no sign of Terrance Loughlin.

Hog braked the vehicle to a gravel-spewing sideways stop. He looked happier than a guy on his wedding night.

"Hop in, dude. Let's nail their asses!"

It sounded like a damn good idea to Mark Stone. He grabbed the open passenger door on the run as Hog fed the heap some gas, and lodged himself into the front seat. The rental sedan barreled down the driveway and through the front gates of An Khom's property.

Bare seconds had elapsed since the limo carrying the

surviving gunmen and their hostage had withdrawn.

Hog emitted a piercing rebel yell and twirled the steering wheel in front of him to send their vehicle into a wide half-turn that took in the opposite shoulder of the road fronting An Khom's before he piloted the sedan into a fishtailing screech that straightened out and sent them rocketing into the night away from Loughlin and whatever was still happening back there on the property of the old black marketeer.

"Some party," Hog growled.

The road and the ride were rough and curvy. Wiley kept the gas pedal floored. The steering wheel bucked in his fists, trying to tear loose, but it was not difficult for the experienced racing driver to keep the vehicle under tight control as they sped along.

No sight yet of taillights.

Damn! thought Stone. *We couldn't have lost them!*

"Any word on the stuff we paid for?" he asked Hog.

Wiley shook his shaggy head without taking his eyes off the road.

They took another curve on two wheels, but the vehicle straightened under Hog's expertise.

"I was hoping you'd know about that," Hog muttered. "I was too busy blowing jerks away who were trying to blow *me* away. Any idea what the hell we walked into back there?"

"Had to be a falling-out between An Khom and his associates, or a competitor moving in."

"Reminded me of the Silver Spur Diner back home on a Saturday night."

"I suppose you didn't have time, either, to get a make on the young lady we're busting our behinds to rescue."

Hog grunted. "Uh-uh. Too damn busy killing."

Hog brought them around another curve. Stone rode the momentum of the turn to the sound of steady curses from Wiley, as he fought to hold control of the vehicle, and the whine of tortured rubber during the turn. Then Mark saw the heartbeat-length glint of their headlights on chrome not fully camouflaged by trees and deeper shadows across the road.

"Brake," Stone snarled. "Trap."

At that moment a woman's scream pierced the night air. Then her scream stopped abruptly, cut off.

"Shit," Hog hissed with feeling.

He braked and jerked the steering wheel sharply to the right.

From across the night-shrouded road, automatic weapons opened fire, pencils of spitting flame stitching the night with meat-seeking projectiles.

Stone heard rounds spang into the rear end of the car, but without serious effect. Hog cut his headlights and braked to a stop across the road, almost opposite the limo. Stone and Hog now had the same cover of night working for them as did the gunmen.

Stone and Wiley clambered from the passenger side of their vehicle away from the gunfire, covered from the incoming rounds by the car's bulk.

The bursts of gunfire continued. The windshield shattered. More rounds punched at the other side of the car, but none of the dozens of slugs found Stone or Wiley, who unlimbered their own weapons and moved, keeping down low, to opposite ends of their car.

Stone and Wiley returned a couple of shots, Stone with his Beretta, Hog with the booming Colt Trooper, then both men pulled their heads down again as answering fire riddled the night.

"I count four of 'em," growled Mark under his breath.

"Five, if one is holding the hostage," added Wiley.

"Four or five, then. They'll spread out in another minute or less, unless we do it first."

"Maybe they'll pull out."

Stone chuckled, ice-cold.

"What an unexpected strain of Pollyanna you've suddenly developed, Hog."

"Huh?"

"They wanted us bad enough to stick around and try again," said Stone, noting that the gunfire had crackled to nothing across the road. He tossed his Beretta to Hog. "Here. Give me a two-count to get clear, then toss a few rounds with each gun. They'll figure we're both answering their fire."

Hog caught the Beretta easily in his left hand.

"What the hell are you up to?"

"I'm going to circle them and close in first."

"Goddamn, guy, you're not carrying a gun!"

"Can't have everything," Stone grunted.

He bolted from the cover of the car in a sideways dive, his dark clothing camouflaging him in the darkness. Stone came out of the loose roll and hustled in a low jog away from the car.

Hog began pulling off rounds right on the numbers, the heavy detonations of the Colt Trooper alternating with a couple of nasty spits from the Beretta before Wiley dodged himself back down behind cover like a jack-in-the-box in reverse, with barely a blink to spare.

More gunfire came from across the road, but by that time Stone was well out of the line of fire, and already moving into position to come in on these gunmen behind the limo from a flank he hoped they had left unprotected. He suddenly wondered if maybe he shouldn't have told Hog to hold his fire after that first burst, but Hog held his fire on his own. *Unless he had been hit.* Mark did not think about that.

He glided soundlessly through the night and came in on the four behind the limo, in the moment after they had again ceased firing.

The air back here was sharp with the stench of cordite, and spent shell casings littered the ground.

Stone saw the captive even as he moved in from behind on the nearest guy, who was toting an AK.

The young woman was Asian and unconscious, a delicate bundle of femininity in Western-style slacks and blouse. Her clothes and the lady herself were in disarray, but at least she was out of the line of Stone's silent attack.

He descended on these goons one-two-three, with martial-arts precision. He delivered the hard edge of his right hand in a slashing descent across the back of the neck of the nearest man. He heard that guy's neck snap like a dry twig, lifted his left arm up and out, and smashed the elbow into the right temple of the second man. The gunman died without making a sound. The two dead men to either side of Stone collapsed, their weapons clattering to the ground, and that was the first sound to alert the other two, who had been aiming AK's across the limo to take out their pursuers.

Both of these gunmen fell back at their first shock of awareness, but in that second Stone moved in on the one to his right. The guy fell back like his buddy, pulling up his AK to target this new threat. Stone's right foot kicked up and out, and the AK flew from the man's stunned fingers. The guy grunted and reached for a concealed piece, but by that time Stone had pivoted on his left foot, bringing his right foot punching out in an arc that caught the guy under the jaw with enough power to snap his neck. As another standing corpse went toppling backward, Stone crouched and picked up the AK-47 the man had dropped. He swung the rifle around to take out the remaining gunman.

Before that could happen, there came another blast from Hog Wiley's Colt Trooper, and the last of these punks pitched forward with the back of his skull blown into bloody pulp.

Stone held onto the AK. He stood up and approached the unconscious figure of the young woman.

Hog Wiley trotted over and glanced admiringly at the young Asian.

"Looks like you won the prize."

Stone lifted her and carried her easily toward the limo.

"Get behind the wheel," he instructed Hog. "Get us back to An Khom's. Fast."

"Roger."

They hustled into the gunmen's limo. Stone propped the young woman in a sitting position on the seat between himself and Wiley. She had about her the subtle fragrance of jasmine and that singular small-boned beauty of the Asian woman, every curve right in place, too.

The limo began moving.

The young woman's eyes snapped open and she looked first to the bearlike profile of Hog, then to Mark Stone. When she recognized that these were not Oriental faces to either side of her, she calmed appreciably.

"Thank you, gentlemen," she said evenly, only because the shock had not set in yet. "I believe . . . you have saved my life."

"Who are you?" Stone asked, point-blank.

"I am An Ling, daughter of An Khom."

Stone sensed that this young woman, no more than seventeen or eighteen, was made of strong stuff, but was vulnerable right now, just the same, after what she'd been through. He felt strong vibrations from An Ling, with uncertainty dominating. He could only hope that once this young woman was on her own, she would be able to come to terms with what had happened to her tonight. If she couldn't . . .

He put the thought away as Hog brought their vehicle over the ridge and toward An Khom's.

Chapter Nine

Less than five minutes had passed since the brief chase and ambush, it had all happened that fast.

An Ling was not his problem, Stone told himself, not beyond taking her back to her father, anyhow.

But this lovely girl did matter to him, strangely, and he suddenly did care very much what happened to her.

An Ling. Lovely name. But so young. And there was Carol, waiting for him, back home...

She abruptly seemed to get very tired, and leaned her head on Stone's shoulder.

Hog steered the limo into the driveway of An Khom's. The main house still burned; the whole top story was in flames.

An Ling did not want to look, so she kept her almond eyes closed. The slim fingers of one graceful hand, surprisingly warm, found Stone's hand and entwined with his fingers for a passing moment of human comfort.

Then Hog braked the limo to a stop halfway to the main house and courtyard.

"We'd better approach on foot. Wouldn't want that damn Englishman to think some of those boys were coming back for another round. And it won't be long before this place is crawling with cops and firemen."

They left the limo and approached the scene of carnage, which had barely changed except for an ancient Chevy pickup parked well away from the blazing house. The pickup was loaded with crates. Terrance Loughlin was securing a tarp to conceal the crates, which looked to contain weapons and explosives. Loughlin saw Stone, Hog, and An Ling, finished his work, and came to meet them.

They came together naturally, by instinct, in the aftermath of battle, without need of shouted signals to each other in the smoky stillness of the night.

Stone, Loughlin, and Wiley all carried captured automatic weapons. Each was ready to kill again, on a heartbeat's notice, if the mission should require it.

But the killing was over, for the moment.

Together, they and An Ling surveyed the scene.

Stone ticked off a rapid body count with grim precision. A dozen guns had fallen in the raid. There might be more inside the house, but if there were, they would be finished now, so much roasted meat inside an oven.

"We'd better pull out," Loughlin suggested. "What we came for is in that pickup. An Khom told me where to find it."

"Where is my father now?" An Ling asked.

In answer to her question, Wiley pointed off in the direction of the manor house.

"There. Oh shit."

Stone turned, along with Loughlin and the young woman, and they were in time to see An Khom emerge from hell itself, a bundle in his arms. After another moment they recognized his burden as a woman's body, thin, almost unbelievably frail, with much of the clothing burned away.

They ran to meet him. Old An Khom was kneeling on the grass when they arrived, some fifty yards from the inferno that had been his home. He laid the woman out upon the grass with gentle hands and knelt beside her, cradling her head.

An Ling cried out and ran to their side.

The older woman was dying, Stone could see that much from where he stood. The combination of her age, her burns, and the rasping of her breathing told the story plainly. She had suffered too much damage, inhaled too much smoke. Her ancient body could not make a comeback. Not this time.

An Khom was bending over her, his ear almost pressed against the withered lips, trying to catch words that were less than a whisper. One trembling hand came up to touch his wrinkled cheek, and when it fell away again, the fingertips were dampened by the old man's tears.

The woman gave a final shudder, let her breath go in a whistling sigh, and she was gone. Whatever had imbued her with the life force seconds earlier had departed.

An Ling held one of the woman's hands and wept softly without looking at those standing around her.

An Khom took a second to compose himself, then regained his footing with an effort. For the first time the old man seemed to show his age, to bow before the years as if they rested on his shoulders. With a flourish he shed his coat and draped it across the lifeless face of the woman on the lawn.

"My wife," he told the men, a tremor in his voice. An Ling rose and he took her in his arms in a sorrowful embrace. Then the old man quickly recovered himself and released her.

"So," An Khom said to Mark Stone, "I owe you a debt— my daughter's life."

He clasped his daughter tightly to him, again. For long

moments they were locked together, weeping softly.

Wily was looking at the dead men sprawled around the courtyard.

"Who are these hairbags, anyway?"

The old man gave a stoic shrug, as if uninterested in the question of exactly who had wiped his family out.

"Perhaps a group of terrorists I once did business with— or else refused to. Who can say?" He scanned the field with watery eyes. "I do not recognize this offal. Paid assassins from the slums and rural provinces, no doubt. They follow orders if their pay arrives on time."

Stone knew the type, of course. He had encountered them in Vietnam, in Laos and Cambodia—everywhere that civil war or revolution had uprooted populations, casting them adrift while teaching them that life was cheap and killing easy and profitable.

Terrance Loughlin cleared his throat. "If there is something we can do..."

An Khom waved the unfinished offer away as if it were a fly buzzing around his face. "You have another job to do, and you have done enough here already. Ours is a business association. You now have what you paid for. Our business is done."

In the distance they could hear the frantic braying of police claxons. Someone in the neighborhood had finally called about the shooting and explosions, summoning what passed for cavalry in Bangkok.

Time was running out, and they could not afford to be discovered there, among a dozen corpses, with those automatic weapons in their hands. The mission would be over before it really started, and a lifelong prison term was definitely not in Mark Stone's plans.

"You be all right?" he asked the weapons dealer, nodding curtly in the general direction of the approaching sirens.

"Yes," An Khom replied, half smiling now. "I know the

captain of police. We have . . . an understanding. I do not expect much trouble. Anyhow, they cannot think that one old man could kill so many well-armed gutter rats."

Stone saw the logic of it, knew that old An Khom already had a fix of some kind working with the authorities. It would explain how he could stay in business, storing weapons at his home. And clearly, now, his only fear had been of those on the wrong side of the law—the sort of men they had surprised here tonight.

Stone's heart went out to him, of course, and he could almost share the old man's sense of loss, but he had seen too much and felt too much throughout his wars to let each death affect him personally now. It was too late for that.

Chapter Ten

Three hours out from Bangkok's city limits they were in the jungle, the capital's crowded streets and lighted avenues a fading memory. The road they traveled was still reasonably broad, but now no longer paved, and with each passing mile it seemed to grow a little rougher in proportion to their distance from the maintenance workers on a civic payroll.

Riding in the open Jeep beside the native driver, Stone gave his undivided attention to the rain forest around them, memorizing landmarks that an untrained eye would overlook in passing, noting the direction of each twist and turn along their path. They would not have to come this way alone if things worked out, but even so . . .

A careful soldier lives to fight again another day. The warrior who ignores his trivia, who bypasses detail in a reckless search for shortcuts, can become a memory in no time.

Stone knew that Hog and Terrance Loughlin, riding in

the back with all their gear, would be every bit as wide awake as he was. These men were pros, and even though experience had led them to have faith in their Laotian contact, you could never be too careful in a combat zone.

Stone smiled, aware that in these days of manufactured "peace" the combat zone was everywhere and included every man among the fighting conscripts. Some men hadn't heard the call yet, and some refused to answer, playing ostrich when the call came, but the time was coming soon for all of them.

And Stone preferred to choose his time and place, select the theater of action where he risked his life. No more, for him, the orders handed down from faceless men on high. No more the commendations written in blood—the blood of other soldiers who had gone before to pave the way with hallowed dead.

Mark Stone was fighting for his own cause, and if the world should choose to stand against him, then the world had best look out. Because Mark Stone was coming through.

The Free Laotian driver was an agent they had used before, but at the end of their drive they would be meeting unfamiliar faces. Mercenaries who sold their services to the highest non-Communist bidder. Today it was Stone and his commandos. Tomorrow...

He put tomorrow and the next day out of mind, and concentrated on the road ahead. On either side the jungle closed around them, treetops meeting overhead to form a natural tunnel, blotting out the sun in places, dappling its light when rays got through at all. Down here, it might be morning, afternoon, or early evening. Days inside the jungle seemed to last forever.

Stone was home again, but he was not at ease. The jungle sights and sounds were all familiar to him, something he had lived through in another time, another war. But there was none of the relaxed sensation that other men experienced on coming home. For Stone, returning to the jungle was like entering a crucible, he had been forged here, tempered in the fire, and more than once he had almost lost his life.

He had come back to risk it yet again, and he would go on coming back, time after time, because, in the final analysis, he had no choice. By profession he was a soldier, and by choice he was a hunter of the lost. Between the two vocations stretched a never-never land where everything ran together, merged, and came out changed somehow. In his younger days he might have blamed it on the jungle, but not now. He knew that every man must make his own killing ground and face the dangers that reside there, every day, in every walk of life.

For Stone the choice was preordained—no choice at all, really. He fought because he could, and therefore had to.

He breathed the forest in, savored every odor and remembered other days. Patrols, and slinking through rice paddies under cover of a velvet night. The days staked out in ambush, when each shadow had a sniper or machine-gun nest, each vine across the trail became a tripwire for explosive booby traps or flying pungi stakes.

And he was going back again, this time to liberate some souls for whom the jungle had involuntarily become a way of life.

The forest held no terrors for Stone or his companions. The disease and quicksand, snakes and lethal insects were acknowledged risks, but they were going in with both eyes open. In another lifetime he had been naïve, but that was long ago, before 'Nam. The first two years of full U.S. involvement in that other war had seen more soldiers killed by insect bites than by hostile fire, but the survivors had learned to cope, to live within the new environment and adapt to it, if not befriend it, then at least declare a grudging truce.

The jungle could consume a man, devour him completely. Or it might just chew him up a little and decide to spit him out again, a hollow shell, devoid of mind or substance. It had done its worst to Stone, and failed. He was the master now, or at the very least a seasoned equal.

He was a survivor.

Like the men he meant to rescue from the living hell of their captivity. For all these lonely years they had hung on, surviving where it was impossible to *live*. As one who had made it out alive, and was now free to live the good life, Mark Stone felt he owed them that, at least. The world outside, which had elected to forget, would owe a damned sight more.

But first he had to bring them out alive, so they would be able to collect their debt.

And that would prove no easy task, if their experience within the past two days was any indication.

In the driver's seat beside him, their Laotian driver was as talkative as a cadaver, answering the rare remarks from Hog or Loughlin with disgruntled monosyllables. Stone tried to think whether he had ever seen the driver smile, and finally recalled a single rare occasion—the Laotian had just drawn his dripping bayonet from the intestines of a dead Vietnamese.

Without a word of warning, they were off the beaten track and jouncing down a narrow, winding trail, with vines and palm fronds dipping low and whipping at the windshield, sometimes etching little lines of blood on sunburned cheeks. A curse came from Hog behind him, and a grunt from Loughlin, as they took the downslope without braking, full speed ahead.

The driver wasn't taking any chances with a tail, but Stone would gladly have turned out to wait and watch the trail behind, in lieu of plunging on at breakneck speed. He checked the Rolex on his wrist and held his tongue. They were ahead of schedule, and he wouldn't mind a chance to check out the terrain before they made their contact with the mercenaries.

He had never worked with either of the men before, and knew them only by their reputations—which were mixed. They were Americans with Vietnam experience, who made a living now by running guns and willing bodies over hostile borders, sometimes stopping off to fight a war along the way, if there was money in it for their pains. They would not deal with Communists, at least not knowingly, but there were rumors of alliances with certain other shady elements who peddled opium and other contraband along with their munitions. In any case, Stone planned to play it safe and not take anything for granted.

After something like three-quarters of an hour, the Laotian started slowing down, almost reluctantly relaxing his death grip on the accelerator. He was sitting at attention now, if such a thing was possible, and scanning the green foliage up ahead as it closed in around the Jeep. Stone realized that this was new to him, and he was doubly thankful that their speed had been reduced.

The clearing came almost as a surprise, and while the driver had clearly been looking for it, there was just a hint of the same relief that Stone felt upon his Asian face as well. He coasted to a halt within a grassy area half the size of a standard football field, but left the engine idling loudly when he parked and set the brake.

Across the clearing, thirty yards away, a Huey helicopter waited for them like a brooding prehistoric insect, giant bubble eyes regarding them impassively, assessing their potential as an evening meal. It was not a comforting comparison, and Stone abandoned it at once, preferring to concentrate on the men grouped around the military surplus chopper.

They were lounging off to either side, almost too casually, as if the automatic rifles slung across their shoulders were for decoration and would serve no deadly purpose. One, an Asian like their driver, leaned against the curving windshield of the cockpit, watching them without emotion on his face. His rifle was a new Kalashnikov, and he kept one hand near the pistol grip now, not taking any chances with the new arrivals.

The other two men were Americans, and Stone recognized them both, although this was the first time they had met. He had researched the pair of them, including some photographs, and he knew enough to write a brief biography about each man at need.

The tall one, lounging near the chopper's open loading bay with one arm draped across the barrel of a sleek M-60 light machine gun, was Deke Hopkins. Over by the chopper's tail, just lighting up a smoke, was Leo Meyers, his partner. Both of them had served in the Marines, with heavy action in 'Nam, and they had passed the test of grim survival. But they had failed, somehow, in peacetime, when it came to laying down their arms and giving up the causes they had fought and nearly died for. They had failed—if it was failure—to adjust within a society where they were vilified as baby-killers, questioned about how many atrocities they had performed or witnessed.

Stone could not have vouched for either man from personal experience, but he had been that route himself, and knew exactly how much pressure had been heaped on returning veterans. Ignored on one hand, and accused on the other—it had been too much for some, and if a few had found release through drugs or aimless violent crime, some others had found a way to make their training pay.

Mark Stone had tried his hand at it, before his personal commitment to a higher cause had led him to forsake monetary profit in pursuit of something higher, more abstract. Like freedom, maybe. Like justice.

Stone dismounted from the Jeep, working out the kinks in his legs a moment before he started off across the clearing. He didn't have to look behind him to know that Hog and Loughlin would be covering his rear, discreetly. This was unfamiliar ground, and these were unfamiliar faces. If all hell broke loose he might go down, but he would not go down alone, by any means.

Meyers seemed to be in charge, and he was ambling out to meet Stone now, his hand extended in a greeting. Stone received it, shook it warmly, held the mercenary's gray eyes with his own. Something sparked between them, and Stone let himself relax a fraction.

It was still too early yet for total trust, but he was on the way. Accustomed to snap judgments, and experienced at gauging men on sight, he sensed that Meyers and Hopkins were all right, at least conditionally. They would not try to stab him in the back or leave him stranded in the middle of the jungle with his neck stuck out a mile.

"You made it." Meyers grinned around his stogie, letting out a cloud of acrid smoke. "We're ready whenever you-all are."

A touch of Georgia there, and that fit with the bio Stone had filed away upstairs. A Southern boy who fought for God and country first, and later for the money.

"Take a minute to offload our gear," Stone told him.

"Let us help you." Almost as an afterthought, Meyers gestured toward the Asian standing by the chopper's nose. "That there's your point man, Lan Vang. He's Free Lao all the way, A-number-one in the bush."

Stone nodded to the Asian, and got a facial tic for an answer. Meyers was on his left as they doubled back to the waiting Jeep, Hopkins falling into step behind them, bringing up the rear. At the vehicle, a cautious Terrance Loughlin had begun unloading duffel bags of gear while Hog stood watch, one hand upon the holstered Trooper on his hip.

Meyers took the bearded hulk in at a glance, and whistled softly to himself.

"They grow 'em big where you come from," he grinned.

The Texan scowled at him and grunted.

"Big and friendly," Meyers amended. "Well, let's tote that barge and lift that bale. It's time to hit the not-so-friendly skies."

Chapter Eleven

The border separating Laos from Thailand is a natural boundary, the Mekong River. Flowing south to meet the China Sea and empty through a delta west of what was once Saigon, the Mekong is familiar to the veterans of Vietnam, a liquid artery of transportation north and south, the scene of many fierce engagements with the Cong and NVA regulars brought down across the DMZ. In that war, it had carried troops and arms both ways, devouring the casualties and sweeping them away for unsung burial at sea. In later wars, all undeclared but no less deadly, the Mekong was a tenuous borderline between opposing forces. Often crossed, but never in the open, it was less an obstacle for the determined warrior than a demarcation point, the last stop before he entered into hell.

Laotians called their land the Lao People's Democratic Republic, but there was precious little democracy inside the jungle nation. All the strings of government were firmly held by members of the Lao People's Revolutionary Party, and the party, in its turn, was dominated by the Pathet Lao guerrilla leadership. Communism was the gospel of the "democratic" state, and its opponents ended up in harsh "reeducation camps," which were the tropical equivalent of a Siberia. The few who came back out again had been "converted" to the new regime, and were anxious to repair the "damage" they had done to "people's government" by speaking freely.

Approximately half the size of Thailand, Laos could boast but one-sixteenth the population of her neighbor state. A large proportion of her people clustered in the capital, at Vientiane, or in the second-largest city, Savannakhet. Out in the wooded countryside, Laotian villages had been systematically decimated since the final victory of creeping Communism to the east, in Vietnam. With fifty thousand armed Vietnamese inside her borders, Laos amounted to a client state, an occupied territory of the new Vietnamese empire, and her natives had become the prey of roving hunter-killer bands that looted freely, raping, robbing, killing at their pleasure. Between the ravages of the Viets and their own government's "reeducation" measures, refugees had turned into the prime Laotian export, flocking into Thailand and Cambodia by the thousands. In an age of Asian population booms, Laos had managed to reverse the trend with a little help from her friends.

Stone knew that roughly two divisions of the occupation troops were stationed to the north, in the provinces of Luang Namtha, Oudomsay, and Phong Saly, to repel the danger of incursion by the Red Chinese. As usual, Communists made shaky comrades in reality, and while the troops of Chairman Mao had tutored Ho Chi Minh and his guerrillas early in the war for Vietnam, it had become a Chinese war of late. The nations, theoretically united in pursuit of Marxist revolution, seemed at times more desperate to annihilate each other than to liberate the proletariat of other lands.

And that was fine with Stone. If fifty thousand of the opposition were committed northward, waiting for a sneak attack from their reputed allies, it meant his men would not have to worry about running into them where it mattered, in the south. Of course, there would be troops enough to bar their way, including more Vietnamese, the Pathet Lao guerrillas, and enough collaborators in the scattered villages to populate a good-sized town if they were all collected in a single place.

Staring past Deke Hopkins and his sleek machine gun, through the Huey's open loading bay, Mark Stone was studying the jungle as it slid by several hundred feet beneath their feet. Night was falling now on both sides of the Mekong, and down there among the trees, beneath the dappled roof of foliage, it would already be dark. The grim nocturnal predators would be awake and prowling—animal and human both—competing for survival in the normal killing cycle of the forest. All but one of them—the human animal—would be abroad to kill for food. But man, with the machinery of war and reason at his fingertips, had found a higher calling: he would kill and kill again for sport, for ideology, for pleasure.

So much for civilization. Stone had been around the world and fought his wars in every climate, without finding any concrete evidence of its existence.

They were coming in with dusk, Leo Meyers at the Huey's delicate controls, and hoping that no hostile eye observed their coming. There was every chance, of course, that they had been picked out already—by the scores of spotters stationed along both banks of the Mekong, or by roving agents deep in the interior of Laos. Either way, discovery could be fatal, and they might be heading even now into a hot LZ, with hostile guns on station, waiting for the signal to blast them out of the sky in flaming wreckage.

It was a chance Stone took each time he climbed aboard

a chopper headed into hostile territory, and it did not frighten him. He was a veteran of many landings behind the lines, and this would not be his last—with any luck at all.

They tried to stretch the safety margin by coming in with darkness, seeking out the clearing that had been selected by Meyers and Hopkins as a landing site. Darkness would impede patrols, if any sought to find them, and it gave Stone's group a fighting chance of getting on the ground and away from the landing zone alive, in case they met with hostile fire on their approach.

He started counting off the heartbeats, never thinking now beyond the moment, as they neared the point of their rendezvous. A clearing, marked by flashlights screwed into the spongy ground, had opened in the canopy of trees below them, and Meyers brought the Huey around in a sweeping circle, running without lights, nothing but the eggbeater sound of his powerful engines to give them away in the jungle's velvet darkness now. They were dipping lower, and Deke Hopkins jacked a round into the chamber of his big M-60, ready just in case the jungle underneath them opened up in roaring flame.

Stone and his companions cocked their CAR-15s, ready now as they could ever be until they reached the solid earth below. Up here they were like sitting ducks, and while they would be able to retaliate against hostile fire to a limited degree, their lives were firmly in the pilot's hands until they left his custody for good. Up here, above the treetops, they were vulnerable in the extreme.

Stone found himself unconsciously holding his breath, and deliberately released it in a long, slow exhalation. They were hovering, descending, perfect targets now for any snipers on the ground or in the treetops, but there were no hostile rounds incoming. Down below he caught a glimpse of movement, and picked out human forms converging on the landing zone.

The touchdown was a rocky one, but solid, without mishap. Hopkins kept his mangler trained in the direction of the figures that were fast approaching, never easing off the trigger as they came within hailing range of the Huey. Only when a reedy voice was raised outside did he visibly relax, and even then, Stone noted, he did not release the trigger of his weapon, but only held it slightly less intently.

"This is it!" Meyers bellowed from the cockpit, shouting to make himself heard above the *chug-chug* of the rotors whirling overhead. Stone nodded to his men and cleared the open loading bay in one fluid motion, relieved to feel the solid earth beneath his feet again.

Behind him, Hog and Loughlin hit the turf, moving out to flank him as they came face to face with what proved to be a two-man reception committee. Their Free Lao guide was moving past them, taking the lead automatically, speaking to the closest of the armed men in his native dialect while Stone and his companions stood by, watching silently.

After a huddled consultation, the guide turned back to face them, motioning to them to follow him.

"This way," he said softly, turning back to leave them in the clear assurance that they would follow his direction without question.

Stone shrugged, and for the moment surrendered himself conditionally into this stranger's care. Time enough later to think about reprisals if it fell apart, if someone turned traitor and started jerking his chain. For the moment there was no damned reason to suppose that these men were other than what they appeared to be: fighters united against the Communists' tyranny that held Laotians underneath a grim, relentless boot heel.

The Huey, with its two crewmen, lifted off behind them, but Stone and his companions were already in the forest, moving along what seemed to be a narrow game trail, following their guides to whatever lay ahead. The forest sounds

and smells were overpowering now, surrounding them as
they moved ever farther away from the slender security of
the clearing. Nightbirds started calling, eerie voices rising
in the night when the apparent threat of the helicopter was
removed from their ancestral jurisdiction. Other animals
were moving stealthily to either side, keeping pace with the
Westerners, taking their scent, perhaps, deciding whether
they were good enough to eat. Once a heavy body veered
away from their line of march, crashing gracelessly through
the underbrush, still unseen, and the three warriors gripped
their weapons tighter, ready for a sudden challenge from
the bush.

Not all the predators were human here, and Stone did
not intend to end his journey in a tiger's belly, or beneath
the crushing hooves of a water buffalo, if he could help it.

After fifteen minutes that felt more like several hours,
they were through the trees and standing all together on a
muddy riverbank. Ahead of them, dark water stretched away
for several hundred yards before it terminated in another
wooded shore.

The river could not hold a candle to the grand, majestic
Mekong, but Stone saw that it was wide enough to block
their passage if their guides had not provided something in
the way of floating transportation. He did not intend to swim
it with the risk of gunners hidden on the other side and
snakes or crocodiles patrolling on the muddy bottom, somewhere out of sight.

His answer made itself apparent in an instant, as he spied
the sampan waiting for them on the bank some paces down.
There was another huddled conference that excluded Stone
and company, then one of the Laotians moved away without
a backward glance, and was soon lost to sight among the
jungle shadows. Lan Vang, the Laotian guide, together with
the nameless one, continued on until they reached the sampan, Stone and his companions obediently in tow. They

climbed aboard, and the Laotian who had greeted them on touchdown took the helm, cranking up a small inboard motor and piloting the rickety craft out into midstream, nosing it northward and running slowly against the seaward current.

Stone and his companions settled in, their weapons handy, as the sampan bore them north. The sky above them was a canopy of stars, the crescent moon a beacon for their mission. Sitting there and listening to the rustle of the water inches underneath him, Stone might have surrendered to some fantasy of peace, but the weapon in his hands reminded him of grim reality, the purpose of his mission.

They were in a war zone, and all of them would have to stay awake, in fighting trim, while they were out here in the open. On the river they were every bit as vulnerable, every bit as exposed, as they had been in the air. More so, in fact, having sacrificed mobility and flight for this snail's-pace mode of travel.

An hour passed in virtual silence, the Laotians speaking seldom, Stone and his commandos not at all. They watched the shadowed banks intently, scanning either side in turn and searching for a light or a movement that might give away an enemy before he had a chance to open fire or telegraph their progress to his base camp in the forest. There were so damned many shadows, there was so much darkness.

There was nothing on the bank or in the forest, at least nothing the naked eye could see without assistance from some night-bright optics, and Mark Stone was wishing for a nightscope when the helmsman hissed a warning to their guide, Lan Vang. The warrior was about to ask him what was happening, but the words died in his throat as he picked out the sound of engines running toward them on the darkened water, growing closer by the moment.

And he recognized patrol boats by their sound, two of them at a minimum, and running south in tandem, sticking to the shores. He could almost pick out their silhouettes against the dim reflection of the moonlight on the water— well enough, in any case, to know that they were closing on a virtual collision course. It was too much to hope that they would overlook the sampan, let it pass them by unnoticed.

As if in answer to his thoughts, a searchlight blazed to life and pinned them in the middle of the river, quickly followed by another, turning midnight on the river into lethal noon.

Chapter Twelve

The twin patrol boats were converging on their sampan, tinny voices hailing them first from one amplifier, then from another, demanding papers, explanation. Huddled in the bow, Stone knew that they could not withstand the most cursory examination, and he knew already what they had to do about it.

Do or die, damned right.

He started counting down, signaling his intentions to the others by a movement of his eyes, a gesture with his flash-suppressor-equipped carbine. They would follow where he led, no doubt about it. And the only question left for Stone was whether they had guns enough and time enough to pull it off. The slim advantage of surprise could only take a man so far, before he had to make it on his own.

The countdown bottomed out at zero, and Stone made his move, already on his knees and sweeping with the automatic rifle as the thought was being filtered through his nerve synapses into action. On his right, Lan Vang was

following his lead, the autorifle that he carried sweeping up
and out across the gunwale of the sampan, its lethal muzzle
seeking targets in the spotlight glare.

Stone was aiming for the searchlight first, and he found
it with a probing, measured burst. The light exploded, wink-
ing out like some cyclopian eye. Over on his right, a burst
from Loughlin or the Laotian found the second spotlight
and put it out of action in a spray of glass shards. An operator
who was tardy in retreating from his station had a major
portion of his brain forcibly externalized, deposited among
his comrades huddling on the deck of their patrol boat, under
fire.

It took an instant for the stunned Vietnamese to react—
long enough, at any rate, for Stone to pick a target on the
bridge of the patrol boat nearest him and slam a three-round
burst into the khaki-covered chest. He saw the uniform
reduced to bloody tatters in the half-light of the moon, and
then the blank-faced corpse was gone, propelled away and
out of sight by the impact of the CAR-15's manglers.

It was in the fan, for damned sure, and the twin patrol
boats were returning fire now, taking time to determine
range and elevation with their light machine guns, feeling
for the sampan, finally finding her without much difficulty.
She obviously had not been built for naval combat, and
Stone knew that she would not remain afloat for long beneath that concentrated fire. Whatever happened now, for
good or ill, would have to happen quickly if they were to
have any chance at all of surviving.

He considered bailing out, but rejected it at once, aware
that they would not survive for half a minute in the water,
with the incoming fire and the prowling crocodiles to pick
them off. The sampan was their only hope—a flimsy one,
from all appearances, but still the best they had.

Stone raked his target vessel with another burst, and was
rewarded as a crewman doubled over and lurched against

the rail with both hands clasped across his punctured abdomen. Stone let him have another single round to finish him—a lethal head shot that almost decapitated him at twenty yards—and then his gun was tracking on, in search of other game.

Their craft was taking hits, and rolling with the punches, but Stone knew that any solid hits below the waterline would spell their doom. No matter what it took, he had to burn the enemy before they started thinking straight enough and long enough to let the human targets go and concentrate upon their weakness, the boat itself.

His life was riding on it, as were all the others', and there was no time for second chances, no margin for error in the game of life-and-death.

Stone watched a gunner slinking out of cover on the rising, falling patrol boat, clinging to the rail and seeking its protection. He got a neat figure-eight burst to the upper back; it clipped his spine below the shoulder blades and left him rolling on the deck, a leaking eel in human form, with no control of anything below the armpits.

His shipmates were dodging all around and over him, some slipping and sliding in the blood that was spreading out across the deck, and almost falling in their haste to find some cover. Stone's carbine was belching short, determined bursts, and punching holes through their ranks whenever someone dallied long enough to make himself a stationary target.

Even so, the gunners on the two patrol boats were laying down an enfilading fire that put the sampan's passengers in clear and present danger of extinction. Bullets chipped the gunwales, scored the decks, and whistled through the little wheelhouse like a heavy-metal cyclone. Any moment now, the hostile gunners might get wise and drop their sights a notch or two—enough to send their vessel to the bottom.

A sudden curse came from Hog, and Mark Stone turned

in time to see him stagger, almost going down. A slug had grazed his temple, sending rivulets of blood coursing down his sunburned cheek and into the forest of his beard—but he recovered quickly, shaking his head like a fighter as he gained his second wind. The blow, so nearly fatal, seemed more to have angered him than anything else, and as Stone looked on, he resumed his duel with the Vietnamese, ripping off short, measured bursts with a kind of controlled ferocity.

On Stone's right flank, a burst from Terrance Loughlin's weapon suddenly deprived one of the patrol boats of its pilot, slamming his lifeless body away from the wheel and dumping him unceremoniously onto the bloody deck. At once his craft began to veer, swinging in and toward the sampan as his crewmates scrambled to regain control in time. They clearly did not relish the idea of ramming their target—at least not while her crew was still alive and firing back.

It took a moment for the Vietnamese to get their vessel in hand, and by the time they managed it, the gap between their own patrol boat and the sampan had been cut in half. The firing now resumed at virtual point-blank range.

Stone was already swinging his CAR-15 back into action on the port side when a bullet took their pilot in the throat. He staggered, falling to his knees, the scream that rose inside him strangled on an internal gush of blood that filled his ruptured throat and burning lungs.

Stone's first awareness of their peril came when the sampan began to veer hard to starboard, swinging freely out to meet the Viet patrol boat on a suicidal collision course. He whipped around, and was in time to see the dying helmsman topple to the deck, his spastic fingers seeking purchase on the bullet-splintered planking, as if trying to drag himself back and into the world of the living by sheer willpower.

The guy was out of it, and Stone dismissed him from his thoughts at once, aware that there was nothing he or anyone could do to help him now. Survival was the top priority, and they would not survive an instant if their ship made contact with the sleek patrol boat.

Stone was moving out, intent on taking the controls himself, but little Lan Vang beat him to it, hurdling the dead man's carcass in time to seize the wheel before the collision occurred. Leaning hard into the work, he pulled them back on course with mere feet to spare, the starboard weapons blazing out directly into hostile faces now. Loughlin might have leaped across the intervening span of water to fight the enemy hand-to-hand.

Stone freed a thermite grenade from his web belt, yanked the pin, and let the grenade fly, the safety spoon departing as the steel egg left his hand. At less than twenty yards, he saw it bounce across the other vessel's deck and spin once before it vanished down the open hatch to disappear below-decks.

An instant later, hell on earth enveloped that patrol boat, brilliant fire erupting from the open hatchway, spilling out like molten lava all across the deck. Thermite coals were burning through the deck and hull in half a hundred places, turning the patrol boat into a drifting, smoking sieve.

A flaming scarecrow scrambled up and through the main door of the pilothouse, both arms fanning the air and leaving little trails of sparks behind, a thin voice keening in agony. He reached the rail and tumbled over, and for an instant Stone could see him as he sank beneath the surface, flames extinguished now, but with the coals of thermite still aglow and eating into him, devouring his flesh.

Aboard the hostile craft, the guns were silent now, and incoming rounds were limited to the vessel on their starboard side. As Stone prepared to face the danger from that quarter next, he spied Hog Wiley, crouched beside the Britisher, both men with frag grenades in hand and cocked to throw.

The double punch was timed and executed to perfection,

both grenades landing on their target, one each in the bow and stern. They detonated in a syncopated one-two smash that rocked the enemy patrol boat, hurling tattered bodies overboard like so much extra ballast. The chatterguns were silent over there, and no more incoming rounds were striking the sampan's deck or wheelhouse. Cautiously, an inch at a time, Stone began to conditionally relax.

The fight was never really over until the body count was made, and they were in the dark on that score, never having had the time to take stock of the odds against them.

On their left, one boat was burning to the waterline, and there could be no question now of anyone on board remaining alive. Off to the right, the second boat was drifting, her stern riding low in the water as if some of the grenade shrapnel might have started a leak somewhere and let the river in. As with the first ship, no signs of life remained on deck, but it would pay to play it safe, and take no chances.

Thrashing sounds below them in the darkened water roused the soldiers and brought them to the starboard gunwale on the double. They finally spotted him—a single gunner thrown overboard by the dual explosions of the frag grenades, now paddling dog-style, trying desperately to keep his gouged and bloodied head above the surface.

Stone shook his head, marveling again at how a people who depended on the rivers for their livelihood could get along without ever learning how to swim. It was amazing— and it also made the obvious solution to his problem that much easier.

"I'll take him," Stone said flatly. The carbine was at his shoulder, and he was sighting down the barrel, already tightening into the squeeze, when the thrashing soldier screamed and disappeared beneath the surface.

A moment later he was back, and thrashing with redoubled fury now, both hands beating at the surface as if he wished not only to remain afloat, but to rise from the water and become airborne. Underneath the surface, his legs— or something else—were churning the dark water into roiling foam.

And Mark Stone knew the answer even as the soldier slipped away, his last scream swallowed by the river. Stone had seen the crocodiles along their course of travel, felt them waiting, watching, and he knew the river had a way of taking care of flotsam, edible or otherwise.

"Mother Nature's garbage disposal," Hog remarked at his elbow. There was the suggestion of a tremor, something like disgust in his voice, and he spat into the flowing current.

In the dappled moonlight, the smoke was rising slowly from their river battlefield. The enemy was vanquished for the moment, but the brief engagement had been expensive for Stone and company, as well. Their pilot was among the dead, and there was every possibility that other boats would be responding swiftly to the sounds of combat, racing even now toward confrontation with the little troop of invaders.

Clearly, there was not a moment to be lost. Stone turned his full attention to Lan Vang, eyes narrowed and voice solemn as he spoke.

"Can you take us on without him?" A toss of the head was enough to indicate their late pilot.

Lan Vang thought about it for a moment, and finally nodded.

"I have some experience with sampans," he replied. "And it is not now far. By sunrise we should reach the place you seek."

By sunrise. Unless they ran into some more patrols. Unless their boat was taking water even now from damage as yet unknown.

A thousand things could keep them from their rendezvous, or slow them down enough to make the mission fruitless. Stone took stock of all the possibilities at once, and nodded back at the Laotian.

"Let's do it," he said simply.

Another moment, while the body of their pilot was disarmed and stripped of all identifying garments, then consigned to the river and the crocodiles. It was the best that they could do for him, and none of them would be expecting any better if their numbers came around on the big wheel of fortune next time out.

You could feel for a man and share the sadness of his passing without letting yourself fall apart and lapse into some kind of disabling sentimentality. Lan Vang never blinked as the body of his countryman slid past beside their sampan, disappearing in a sudden swirl of ripples, one foot dragging along the surface for a moment before the croc secured a tooth-hold and took him all the way under.

It was the law of the jungle: the fit and cunning would survive; the rest would die and feed the cycle, keep it going in perpetuity. As for Mark Stone, he didn't think of himself as some kind of perpetual-motion fighting machine, and he damned sure never saw himself in terms of immortality—but he was determined to do *this* job to survive *this* time.

This was all he had. It was the present, past, and bloody future all rolled into one, and Stone had bought his ticket to the end of the line.

Chapter Thirteen

Their journey up the river had become a waking nightmare, every man among them tense, expectant, clinging to his weapon, white-knuckled, while he eyed the night and looked for hostile shadows. Every sound warned of potential danger, and the sense of their exposure, of their naked vulnerability, was redoubled for Stone and his companions in the wake of their firefight with the Viet patrol boats.

Time was short, no doubt about it. Even if the dying enemy had lacked the time to radio for help, patrols would be expected to check in at frequent intervals. And when they missed—perhaps not at the first check, or even at the second, but sooner or later—other troops would be dispatched to find them. They would come in greater numbers, bearing arms, and if Stone's little troop was still upon the water when they came...

Stone did not want to contemplate the consequences. There were risks enough ahead for all of them, without borrowing imaginary trouble in advance. They would meet the next wave, if and when it came, as they had met the first. With everything they had.

The hours seemed to drag interminably, and there was pinkish color in the eastern sky before they finally reached their landing point without another incident. Stone felt the sampan slowing. Startled out of an uneasy slumber, he glanced all around him quickly, making sure that they had not run into further trouble as he dozed.

The jungle must be getting to him, working the old magic on him once again. In 'Nam, he had been able to doze off anywhere, anytime, catching a few seconds of respite here and there, when he could, between the killings. Now, after their brief reentry to the killing zone, he felt the same old patterns coming back, more as if by instinct than from training and long hours of practice.

At the helm, Lan Vang was guiding them in toward the spongy bank, and in the gray of early morning, Stone could make out the figure of a man waiting for them where the forest met the shore. He was much like their guide in appearance; he wore the same fading fatigues, and carried an automatic rifle over his shoulder in the same fashion, muzzle down, against invasion by the morning dew.

Lan Vang called out to the newcomer, his voice carrying across the expanse of water like a shout, although he barely seemed to whisper. On the bank, his opposite number waved them in, a brief hand signal indicating that their landing zone was cold, devoid of enemies at present.

Stone was ready when the sampan nudged against the mossy bank, and an agile spring carried him over the gunwale into knee-deep water, splashing swiftly toward the shore. Hog and Loughlin were close behind him, all three carrying their weapons at the ready.

The newcomer scrambled aboard for a hurried conversation with their guide before Lan Vang himself disembarked. Another moment, and the Free Laotian fighter was pushing the sampan off and into deeper water, with the new man still aboard and at the helm.

"He will dispose of it downriver," Lan Vang explained to all of them, his voice flat, matter-of-fact. "The boat is of no use to us with bullet scars. Too easy for patrols to spot us."

"Right." And from Hog Wiley's tone, the others knew that he was none too happy with the thought of being stranded in the middle of the jungle, miles from any village, without means of taking to the river as a form of transportation.

"So, we walk," Stone said, and almost before the words had left his lips, Lan Vang was past them, into the rain forest, setting their course at what amounted to a jogging double-time.

Falling in behind their guide, Stone knew he did not have to stress their need for haste. Already the Vietnamese patrol boats might have been discovered, taken under tow, and new patrols on land and water might be fanning out to find the killers. They were running out of time, and the moments they wasted standing on the riverside and jawing could be better used in putting miles behind them, drawing nearer to their target area.

The forced march quickly found its pace, became almost a marathon as they fell into single file. Lan Vang preceding Stone, with Loughlin next and Hog Wiley bringing up the rear. Forest giants dwarfed them on all sides, trees rising up out of the spongy ground to sweep against the sky and blot it out, lianas trailing earthward like long green whiskers.

The air was hot, stifling, with humidity approaching ninety percent. Intermittent rain would fall, but it would never ease the heat, merely plastering their damp fatigues against their skin, making it that much easier for flies and mosquitos to find their fleshy targets. If the forest hid them from the broiling sun, it also kept them trapped inside the pressure cooker, steaming slowly as they plodded over ground that sucked and clung around their boots, making every step cost twice the effort that it would on normal ground. Within a hundred yards the muscles in their legs were crying out for rest, but rest was not an option for the manhunters. Time was of the essence, and they could not waste a moment— not to eat or rest, or to void their bowels—if they had any hope of reaching the strike zone on schedule, of pulling off their mission under the self-imposed deadline.

Everything was riding on their timing now, and they were already running behind, due to their clash with the patrol boats on the river. They would have to make up that time, or run the risk of having made the trek for nothing.

Once again the sights and sounds and smells were closing in around Mark Stone, transporting him into another time and place. It was so much like 'Nam—and why not? Laos and Vietnam had once been the same country—Indochina— finally divided by the politicians rather than by nature. Artificial boundaries might now lie between the countries and their warring tribes, but trees and plants and animals could read no maps; they put down roots at will, wherever the climate would support them, and there they flourished in a riotous panorama of life and death, birth and decay.

The jungle carries with it certain odors that a man, having once sampled them, can never quite forget: the smell of stagnant water, breeding pestilence; the scent of under-growth as it begins to molder, turning into natural fertilizer for the larger growths; and yes, the smell of *death,* an all-pervasive miasma that hangs across the forest like a pall, almost visible.

Stone caught the scent, but he was not intimidated by it. He had contributed to it himself, the night before. He had helped to feed the cycle, and he would be feeding it some more, one way or another, before his mission reached an end.

The denizens of the jungle were giving them a wide berth

as they traveled, though the soldiers took extreme care to move quietly through the underbrush. Living things in tune with the routine of the rain forest could sense their presence and smell them out without crackling twigs and clanking hardware to alert them. They would know, and pass the silent word along, alerting others that life must pause, delay its cycle, while the mutual enemy was near.

Another enemy was waiting somewhere up ahead, and Stone was concentrating on the human animal as he kept pace with their guide. There had been no intelligence as to the size of the guard force they would find around the prison camp, what kind of backup those Viets might have from the local Pathet Lao guerrillas—in short, none of the data that could finally prove vital to their mission.

An hour from the river, Lan Vang froze suddenly, dropping to a crouch some yards ahead of Stone, who instantly froze in his tracks, his finger on the trigger of his CAR-15.

He heard it even before Lan Vang had a chance to telegraph the warning back along the line in silent hand signals. There were footsteps up ahead, and men were closing on them from an oblique direction, crashing through the undergrowth and making little effort to conceal their passage as they came.

Stone crouched down, and knew the others at his back were now alert and ready without looking at them. They were pros, and they would take care of themselves. Ahead of him, Lan Vang was worming his way backward, an inch at a time, taking special care now not to make any sound whatsoever as he retreated.

The sounds of the enemy were close now, and Stone imagined that he could reach out and part the ferns in front of him to touch them if he wished. Their voices, never bothering to whisper, were loud enough to make him flinch. He knew that if his own men had made this much noise, they would be dead meat by now.

These crashing footsteps and the booming voices in the forest were those of his enemies. They moved with confidence because the land was theirs, an old, familiar friend, and they could not conceive of enemies invading it. From their dialect he knew that they were Pathet Lao, the country's own equivalent of the Viet Cong, glorious victors in the brutal "war of liberation" that had left their land enslaved by the Vietnamese. Veterans of a war that spanned the generations, these were soldiers born to killing, but softened now by a kind of uneasy peace. They believed themselves untouchable on this side of the river, and they took no pains to hide their passing from the eyes and ears of the forest.

Stone could have killed them, set up an ambush across the game trail they were following and cut them down before they had a chance to break formation—but he let them pass. They were his enemies, but at the moment they were not his targets. He was here on a rescue mission rather than a search-and-destroy.

Later, while they were withdrawing, there might be a chance to strike a blow against them. For the moment it was wise to let them pass along their noisy way and wait till their sounds had faded into distant silence.

Lan Vang was finally satisfied, and rising from his crouch, he proceeded on along the trail as if there had been no interruption.

The terrain that they traversed was constantly changing, only the jungle cover remaining constant as they put miles between themselves and the river that was their lifeline, their path of escape in case of mortal danger. Now they might scale a cliff, and moments later find themselves descending an embankment on their backsides. Once they had to ford a hip-deep river, each of them aware that gunners on the other bank could pin them down and cut them all to ribbons with a single concentrated burst of fire, leaving them to feed the eels and crocodiles downstream. And yet they made it, never daring to relax as they overcame each new obstacle. They held together, following their Free Laotian guide deeper into the clinging, choking forest of his homeland, moving on into a confrontation with the enemy they had come to face, the allies they had come to rescue.

It was afternoon before Lan Vang stopped dead in front of Stone and raised his hand to call a halt. They were atop a knoll, still wooded, but with gaps between the trees which were devoid of choking undergrowth, affording them a field of fire if they should be attacked. It was high ground, the jungle sloping off on either side, and Stone immediately knew their guide had found the base campsite that he was searching for.

"We stop here, wait for night," he told them as he sat down cross-legged on the grass.

"How far?" Stone asked him simply, knowing there would be no need for more elaboration of his question.

"Close. Maybe two clicks . . . that way."

A thumb jerked up and backward, over his left shoulder, in a generally northerly direction.

"And you're sure it's still there?" Loughlin prodded.

Lan Vang could only shrug and shake his head.

"All were there a week ago," he told the Britisher. "I have not seen them since, but I think they do not move away so soon."

"You think," Hog Wiley grumbled, sitting down slowly, his back against a tree, with the CAR-15 upright between his knees.

The Laotian shrugged again, but did not answer. Stone knew that his information might be out of date, but there was nothing they could do about it now. There was no such thing as late-breaking news out of occupied Laos; a manhunter had to take the morsels he could get and use them to his best advantage, praying all the time that weather or some whim of the commanding officer would not remove his targets long before he reached them.

If the camp was gone, then they had come for nothing, wasting time and risking life in vain. But if the prisoners were there, then it would be worth anything to take them out alive and kicking, right from underneath the noses of their Vietnamese tormentors.

Stone sat down to wait for darkness, and made his mind a blank against the nagging doubts and questions that pressed in upon him in a rush. They would all be answered in due time, when darkness fell. Until that time, Stone nodded, dozed . . . and finally slept. His dreams were dark, and filled with blood.

Chapter Fourteen

Another jungle night, the crescent moon a fraction larger now, but still almost invisible among the looming trees and undergrowth. There would be little light to go by in the forest—and perhaps too much inside the prison camp itself.

Mark Stone was crouching in a clump of ferns, Hog Wiley close beside him in the humid darkness. Terrance Loughlin and Lan Vang would both be in position by this time, some fifty yards to either side and ready to provide covering fire at need. It was a crude encircling maneuver, and an incomplete one at that, but it was the best they could hope to accomplish under the circumstances.

Just ahead of them, across another thirty yards of obviously manmade clearing, lay the prison camp. A fire was burning in the center of the compound, giving them distorted shadow-views of everything that lay within, and there were several lights that Stone identified as running off a generator housed somewhere inside the camp.

The hour was approaching midnight, earlier than Stone liked, but they would need the darkness for their cloak as they retreated with the prisoners, and a raid at dawn would not allow them time to make a getaway. It would be now, or not until tomorrow night—and every extra day spent in the jungle near the camp increased the odds of their discovery and capture—or their deaths.

Hog and Stone were scanning, memorizing details of the camp from where they crouched, invisible in darkness. Stone had marked the sentries—three of them, circling the long perimeter irregularly, sometimes doubling back upon their steps to cover a particular stretch of ground twice before moving on. It was an effective system, but still far from foolproof. Designed, from the look of it, to make sure no one got out of the camp, it might still allow one grim, determined warrior to get *in*.

The camp itself was typical of other villages and camp-sites that Stone recalled from his tours in Vietnam. Buildings carved out of the living jungle, built with lumber at a min-imum, thatched roofs in place of shingles. Crude structures, certainly, but nothing new to the Vietnamese who spent their off-duty hours inside, away from the steamy jungle heat. They would be country boys, most of them—and that meant jungle dwellers, whether north or south, accustomed to the rustic way of life and all its hardships. They would be at home beneath the thatch, if not exactly comfortable.

There was nothing in the way of fencing to prevent his entry. They were counting on security inside the camp, and then relying on the jungle as a sort of natural obstacle course to slow the prisoners down in case of an escape. It was a workable plan, but it did not provide for any sort of outside interference. There were weaknesses, and Stone would have a use for each and every one of them before the night was done.

A quick count of the buildings showed him a lighted

command hut, away to his left, or north. Two barracks buildings, long and low, each capable of housing twenty men, were close together near the CP, and three more were stationed on his right, in a sort of semicircle that reminded him of covered wagons positioned to ward off Indian attack. The generator hut was near the southern barracks grouping, and his target of the moment, the confinement cages, were dead-center in the compound, with some other shacks of undetermined use nearby.

He pondered the number of soldiers that the camp was clearly able to accommodate. From the number of crude bamboo cages in the camp, he would have thought the number of Viet troops excessive for the job they had to do. No matter, they were here, and he would have to work around them if he didn't want to go right through them. Given a choice, Stone would prefer to work within the darkness, slip his target personnel away before the enemy knew what he was doing. But if it came down to a fire-fight . . .

Well, the four of them would simply have to do the work of ten men each. No sweat.

Like hell.

"You sure about this?" Hog asked him in a whisper, close beside him on his left.

"No way around it," Stone replied. "It's what we're here for."

"Roger that. But watch your ass in there. I can't see everything at once."

Stone grinned at his burly friend in the jungle darkness.

"I'll do that," he promised. "Just see to it that you stay awake back here, and keep in touch."

"You got it, man."

He waited for the nearest guard to make his pass, then double back upon his track, repeating twenty yards of scanning with a sluggish step before returning to his course and heading off behind the nearest barracks on the right. It was now or never, and Mark Stone was ready for it, primed to go.

Like all the others, he was decked out in a suit of jungle camouflage, face and hands blackened with combat cosmetic creams. He held the CAR-15 at the alert, but he was hoping that he wouldn't have to use it, for a single shot would bring the whole encampment down upon him at the double. This time, he had his silencer-equipped Beretta for the job.

It was to be a silent probe, reconnaissance in depth, with contact made among the target personnel if time and circumstances should permit. He would touch base, get the lay of the land from inside the camp, and then withdraw to plan the final thrust with Hog and Loughlin, leaving time to pull it off before dawn.

A simple plan, but then that kind always worked best, if you got the chance to execute it without interruption from the enemy. A damned big *if,* all right, and one that Stone knew he could never count on in a combat situation.

Moving like the night wind, making no sound, he left concealment, gliding with the shadows as he crossed the open ground in one concerted rush. He gained the shadow of the nearest barracks, and was within better viewing range of the confinement cages now, almost able to pick out the forms of the P.O.W.'s huddled inside, apparently asleep. They were within his grasp, not twenty yards away, but if things went sour now, that twenty yards might as well be two hundred miles of bad country road. Those twenty yards could get him killed, and Stone did not need a reminder of just how quick and easy death could be, out here in the middle of godforsaken nowhere.

Another countdown, waiting while yet another sentry finished off his round and disappeared from sight. Could he have stopped, back there behind the generator hut, to lie in wait and watch for any movement in the camp? Stone saw no sign of him, but still . . .

He shook the jitters off and made his move, trusting to experience, his combat sense, as he made the rush, sliding in beside the closest of the cages like a runner coming home with fractions of an inch to spare.

Inside the cage a human figure snapped awake, came upright with a little startled sound. No spoken words, but there were bright eyes staring at him in the night, reflecting firelight from the bonfire in the middle of the barracks cluster, taking everything about him in at once and trying to digest it on the spot.

"A . . . American?"

The voice was like a croaking toad's; it seemed to come from miles away instead of inches, and Stone recognized the signs of dehydration—in the voice, and in the P.O.W.'s thin, emaciated face.

The guy was being starved . . . not quite to death, but damned sure close enough. And there were signs of other punishment as well, cuts and bruises, marks of beatings, old and new. Most of them new.

"Right. You Bradford?"

The scarecrow shook his head, and seemed almost exhausted by the effort as he raised a hand and hooked one thumb back and over a bony shoulder, toward the next cage in line.

"Over there. I'm Wilcox, Robert T. Serial number 570848351."

"Well, hang on, Wilcox, Robert T. We're getting out of here tonight."

"No shit?"

The captive's voice was weak, but even so, the disbelief showed through. It was as if the man suspected he was speaking with a waking dream, a shadow without substance. He could carry on the conversation, but he wasn't buying it, not yet.

Stone hoped that his delirium had not progressed too far, that he could still be salvaged in the time allotted for their break and getaway. There would be no time for psychoanalysis along the trail, no time at all for cajoling and persuading the P.O.W.'s to come along of their own volition. It would be hit and run, the devil take the hindmost. And Stone had no intention of leaving anyone behind him in that living hell.

"Hang tight," he told the man inside the cage. "And just be ready when we spring you. It's a one-shot deal."

"I read you."

And he did. There was something in the voice that spoke to Stone of substance, as if the man were clawing his way up and out of an unpleasant trance, waking from the nightmare to recognize reality.

Stone moved along until he reached the second cage in line, and crouched there, melting into its irregular shadow as another sentry passed him at forty yards, circling the campsite's perimeter. If the guy glanced over, saw anything suspicious about the cages...

But he didn't, and another moment saw him on his way. Stone turned his full attention to the man inside the wooden cell—and saw that he was not about to answer any questions.

If the first P.O.W. had been obviously mistreated, this one had been totaled. He was still alive, but barely, clinging to the thread of life by guts alone, without apparent reason. Beaten savagely about the face and naked abdomen, he was a mass of welts and bruises, scarcely recognizable. Nora Bradford would not know her husband in this shape, and she might not have the chance, judging from his condition.

Stone looked him over briefly in the filtered firelight,

noting bloodstains on the tatters of his shirt and fatigue pants. It took another moment for him to see the bandaged stub of what had been his left hand, severed at the wrist in a crude amputation, obviously cauterized by fire.

Stone's gorge was rising, but he fought it down. His rage could be an enemy, making him careless, reckless in his urge to hit back at the enemy, and if there was one thing he could not afford right now, it was mistakes.

There was no time to ponder whether the amputation had been medical or strictly punitive. Either way, it was sloppy and probably infected, in spite of the cauterization. Bradford might be dying even now, and from the look of him, he might not mind the last release of death.

But Stone had not come here to make the last decision for him. He would take the wounded soldier out of there, if he could find a way. Any way at all. If he could not . . . well, damn it, there would be some time to think about alternative solutions when they got that far.

The voice beside him, almost at his elbow, startled Stone, made him jump.

"The bastards worked him over something fierce," a Georgia accent told him from the cage adjoining Bradford's. "Said the hand was the price of attempting to escape. Lousy fuckers."

"How long ago?"

"Four days . . . no, five, I think. It's getting kinda hard to keep track of the weeks, ya know?"

Stone nodded solemnly.

"They've got some calendars where we're going," he assured the prisoner. "Who am I talking to?"

"John Mandrell. But all my saviors call me Jack."

"All right, Jack. I've got some backup, and we mean to get you out of here—tonight. You just sit tight while I get back to them, and we'll be coming in for all of you before you know it."

"Sounds real good. Hey, listen—"

Stone hesitated, already half-turning to leave when the caged man called to him.

"Yeah?"

"You wouldn't kid a fella?"

"No damn way."

"All right. I reckon I'll be waitin' for you, then. No place to go, ya understan'?"

Stone flashed the gutsy P.O.W. another smile and doubled back along his former route, pausing beside Wilcox's cage long enough to pass another reassuring word, catch a terse monosyllable in return. Clearly, Mandrell would be their best bet of the three, but even he was in atrocious shape from hunger, dehydration, and torture. None of them would be setting any land-speed records on the getaway, and that meant a greater likelihood of a fighting withdrawal through the jungle.

Great. Exactly what Stone did not want to happen.

Well, they had all come this far, and they would see it through. He owed that much to the men inside the bamboo cages, any way it played. And if they all went down together in the jungle . . . well, at least they would have made the effort.

He was about to make his move, break for the jungle treeline and the point where big Hog Wiley would be crouching, waiting for him, when the scraping sound of feet on sod alerted him to danger at his back. The soldier pivoted, swinging his Beretta up to face the sentry, deviating from his normal rounds, who was approaching him from less than twenty feet away.

The enemy was startled, but it only reached his eyes, and didn't seem to interfere at all with the professional way he swung his AK-47 up and into combat position. The Vietnamese had a finger on the trigger, hesitating for a heartbeat and deciding whether he should kill at once or try to take another prisoner for their collection.

Stone never gave the bastard time to think about it. With a feral growl, he pressed the trigger of his silenced Beretta, and the man wailed as he fell.

It was in the fan, damn it, and they would all just have to buckle down and eat it now.

The raid was on.

Chapter Fifteen

It had taken maybe half a second to complete the kill, but the sentry's death cry was enough to raise the camp and bring the enemy against them. Long enough, perhaps, to seal their fate unless Stone acted very swiftly, with some backup from his troopers in the jungle fifty yards away.

Troops were already boiling out of the barracks to the north, and voices were raised among the others, letting him know that their compatriots would not be long in falling out themselves. A door banged open in the command hut, yellow light flooding out into the compound and competing with the flickering light from the bonfire. A male figure was briefly framed in the doorway, then someone remembered the rules of jungle warfare and ducked back out of sight, extinguishing the light at once.

No matter, Stone had seen them, and he knew they would be barking orders in another moment, marshaling the troops into a counterattack formation. He would quickly have a chance to find out just how many hostiles the compound contained, but the prospect wasn't one he looked forward to.

Stone caught another hint of movement in the now-dark doorway of the CP, and fanned a short burst from his carbine in their general direction, knowing as he squeezed the trigger that he would be wasting ammunition. Still, if he could keep their heads down for a moment longer, give them something to fear besides fear itself, he might just have a chance to pull it off.

He doubled back, forgetting the dead sentry and his all-too-active comrades for the moment, concentrating on the prisoners inside their bamboo cages. Each cage had a single narrow door, each held in place by padlock and chain, but there was no time to attempt to pick the locks.

"Stand back!" Stone barked to Jack Mandrell, leveling his carbine as he spoke and squeezing off a burst that tore the lock and chain apart. Mandrell hit the door a second later, plowed on through, and executed a sloppy somersault before ending upright on his knees.

Stone was betting on Jack Mandrell, hoping his first impression had been accurate. The captive seemed more alert, stronger than either of his comrades, and there was a chance, however slim, that he could help them all get out of there alive.

Mandrell wasn't waiting around for instructions from his deliverer. Instead he leaped past Stone, stumbling, almost losing his control of his weakened legs, but he reached the fallen sentry's AK-47, and had it in his hands before the first reacting troops knew what was happening inside the compound.

Stone was satisfied, already turning toward the cage where Alex Bradford was confined. Two more to go, and even if they couldn't help him pull it off, he might have shaved the odds a fraction by taking Mandrell onto the combat team.

The captive's borrowed weapon opened up, and Stone

responded with his own, aiming at the lock on Bradford's cell, silently praying that they would be granted time, luck, and breathing room.

Hog Wiley saw the sentry coming, but there was absolutely nothing he could do about it unless he chose to open fire from hiding, waste the guy, and let Stone take his chances in the open with the camp alerted. If he sat back and waited, there was still a chance the man might pass Stone by, overlook him somehow, or—

Except he didn't pass Stone by, didn't overlook a thing. The camp was blazing into life, spotlights coming on from over by the CP, others by the barracks on the south perimeter. They swept the jungle first, and Hog crouched lower in the undergrowth, instinctively, knowing even as he did it that they could not see him. Troopers were responding to the gunfire, turning out in assorted phases of undress, but none of them forgot their weapons in the scramble.

Stone was dead—unless he got some help before they zeroed in on him. Unless a timely blow from somewhere on the camp perimeter distracted opposition soldiers and alerted them to other dangers in their rear.

Hog raised his CAR-15, sighting quickly, smoothly down the barrel, lining up a clustered group of targets by the nearest barracks. They were waiting for instructions, and the hesitation sealed their fate before they got a chance to act.

He squeezed the trigger gently, sent a measured burst among them, watched them fall apart. Two of them tumbled to the left, a third to the right, and Wiley missed the fourth completely, sending him scurrying back inside the flimsy barracks, seeking shelter there. Outside, his late companions writhed upon the ground, their vital juices spilling from the ugly wounds his bullets had opened in flesh and khaki fabric.

Tracking on, he spied a sniper over by the generator hut,

about to draw a bead on Stone and the little clutch of
P.O.W.'s. Hog loosed a burst that nearly cut the guy in
two and left him lying on the ground, thrashing feebly.

On his flanks, Loughlin and the squat Laotian were
weighing in with cover fire from their concealed positions,
giving Stone's opponents something else to think about,
picking some of them off where they stood, driving the
majority back and under cover for the moment. Half a dozen
of the armed Vietnamese were still inside the nearest barracks, starting to return fire now from slits cut in the walls,
and Hog decided it was time he took the situation in hand.

He freed a thermite grenade from his web belt, pulled
the pin, and let the egg fly, all in one fluid motion. It struck
the thatch roof of the barracks, hung there for a heartbeat,
and exploded just as it began to roll along the downslope.
Instantly the long, low hut became a white inferno, coals
of thermite spewing out in all directions, catching on the
other barracks huts nearby, igniting them as well. Inside
the blazing hut, someone was screaming hopelessly, and all
the gunfire was extinguished as another type of flame took
top priority.

Hog waited, and a moment later men came spilling out
of there, some of them burning like torches, others jostling
past them in their haste to save themselves. He raked their
ranks from end to end and back again the other way, emp-
tying his magazine before he finished, dropping half a dozen
of them in their tracks and penning several others up to die
within the raging flames.

A ghastly silence overcame the burning barracks, the
hungry whooshing of the flames devouring every other sound.
No more hostile fire from that direction, no more life inside,
and it was time to worry now about the enemy in other
quarters, just as deadly, still alive and fighting.

He had given Stone a breather, momentarily, but the

game was far from over, and as he reloaded, Hog was still not sure which way the odds were falling.

Commander Chong Tri Minh was frightened, disbelieving. For the first time within living memory, he felt his control of a combat situation slipping through his fingers, and the feeling was unsettling. It emasculated him, left him ashamed and quaking where he lay, pressed against the outer wall of his command hut in the firelit darkness.

He had no idea what was happening in his compound, why his men were firing wildly, blindly into the darkness. Someone had triggered a burst—he had recognized the telltale sound of a CAR-15—but still, he had no way of knowing who, or why.

If they were under attack, it might be anyone. Hmong. Cambodians. Thais.

Americans?

He scowled at the idea, dismissing it from his mind. Americans were weaklings; they let the United Nations do their talking for them, and for years now they had done nothing *except* talk. Had not the Vietnamese People's Republic already defeated the American paper tiger once in combat? They had driven it back eastward across the Pacific with its tail tucked between its legs, and someday they would wipe the last traces of its presence out of all Southeast Asian nations. But for now, Commander Chong had more immediate concerns—such as personal survival.

Someone, somewhere, was trying to kill him, or so it appeared. The bullets that had missed him so narrowly might have been stray rounds, of course, his own men firing blindly at shadows, but still—he could take no such thing for granted here and now, with gunfire tearing the night apart all around him.

He drew his pistol, taking some marginal comfort from

its familiar presence in his fist, and began worming his way along on his belly, crawling from his CP in the general direction of the small communications hut. If there were some hostilities afoot, he would have to find out about it from Command Central. And if this was nothing but some kind of border feint by the Thais, he would surprise them with a call for reinforcements from the north.

As he wormed his way along, he wondered whether any reinforcements could arrive in time to help him. They were miles away, at Tran Li, and at night it would be slow going in the jungle, even with the incentive of combat to spur them on.

Or slow them down, he thought, and quickly put the thought away. It was disloyal of him to question the integrity and courage of Vietnamese freedom fighters; but still, he had seen enough of them in action here in Laos to know that they would usually rather run than fight. The army was becoming lazy, and while still capable of brutality on occasion, troops were seemingly more interested in rape and plunder than in spreading revolution for the motherland, in memory of Ho Chi Minh.

Halfway to the communications hut, he saw the muzzle flashes in among the trees, outside his own perimeter, and knew that he was truly under hostile fire. He had no way to count the weapons from his prone position, with restricted visibility, but there were several, firing now in unison, scattering his troops and leaving casualties strewn about the field like broken mannequins.

He picked up speed, and was almost there when the communications hut exploded, the force of the concussion picking him up and hurling him backward, airborne, his senses reeling.

Stone dragged the door af Alex Bradford's little bamboo cage open, reached inside, and hauled the P.O.W. out

into the compound. Moving swiftly, he tracked on, blasting
the lock off Wilcox's cage and edging back as Wilcox found
freedom on his own, emerging on all fours, a giant spider
crawling from its burrow, trapped and cringing in the firelight.

They were out of time, and now the enemy was closing
on them, even under the continuous cover fire from his
commandos hidden in the trees. Mandrell had dropped a
couple of them in their tracks, cackling as the bullets ripped
them open, but suddenly his gun was empty, leaving him
to scramble back and search the corpses for extra magazines.

Snipers were finding the range, bullets eating up the night
all around them, and Stone knew the time had come to move
or die. Another moment here, no more, and their position
would be overrun.

He spotted two Viets attempting to outflank them, and
met them with a burst that swept them both away and left
them sprawling on the turf. A third, about to take the same
approach route, now thought better of it, diving back for
cover as Stone chased him with another triple-punch.

Stone grabbed for another magazine to feed into the
CAR-15 when their position was overrun sooner than he
expected at a moment when Mandrell also held an empty
weapon.

A half-dozen N.V.A. regulars in various stages of undress had seen Stone and Mandrell come up empty, and had
decided to close in fast and capture the escapees and Stone
alive. The regulars were too cocky, and one of them even
chuckled to his comrades as they advanced.

Stone and Mandrell assaulted the troopers as if on a
prearranged signal, with enough surprise and ferocity to gain
them a margin for survival.

Stone flayed sideways with the CAR-15 and knocked
three of their rifles aside in one punching arc. He followed
through with a hand-heel punch to the bridge of the nearest

soldier's nose, sending shards of bone into his brain. Stone's right boot lashed out and caught the next soldier in the crotch, smashing genitalia all the way up into this creep's throat. The guy groaned and collapsed to his knees, puking. Stone stepped forward as the third soldier attempted to bring his rifle around again to fire. Before he could, Stone smashed the guy in the throat, crushing his windpipe. The man dropped his weapon and grabbed at his throat, choking. Stone slugged him in the forehead with the butt of the CAR-15, killing him. Then he clubbed the kneeling soldier to death with one hard bop across the back of his head with the rifle butt.

Stone turned to see Mandrell pin one N.V.A. regular to the ground, bashing the guy's head over and over against a tree trunk until blood bubbled from the soldier's ears, nose, and mouth, and Mandrell knew he was dead.

Another soldier brought up his rifle to shoot Mandrell. Stone came up behind the guy and wrapped the CAR-15 around his throat. He twisted the rifle brutally and heard the man's neck snap above the other sounds around them.

Mandrell shouted a warning and Stone turned, still propping up the dead soldier with the carbine under his throat, as the last of these six regulars tracked his own rifle to open fire. Stone shoved the body he was supporting, and the man with the broken neck tumbled into the soldier aiming at Stone. The guy lost his balance just long enough for Stone to unsheath the knife on his webbing and flick it fast and true to pierce the man's heart before he could fire. Stone hurried over to retrieve his knife, and wiped off the blood on the dead soldier's tunic. Then he returned the knife to its sheath.

It had all happened in less than thirty seconds.

Mandrell found another full clip on one of the dead men, and Stone finished reloading.

It was a losing game, no doubt about it. He called out to Mandrell, urging him to hurry up, for Christ's sake, and

help him get the others out of there. The prisoner responded
with a crisp "Affirmative"—some of the military starch still
present under stress—and he was turning back to help when
thunderous explosions started marching through the night,
surrounding them, sending the camp to hell in a hurry.

Stone hugged the ground, clenching his teeth and riding
out the concussion, waiting for the doomsday drumroll to
wash over them.

Chapter Sixteen

Colonel Alex Bradford heard the automatic fire from miles away, a ringing, hammering, staccato counterpoint to all the humming in his skull. Dizzy, out of focus, he was reeling, now unable to stay upright, cursing the darkness that was threatening to envelop him.

There was something . . . he could not quite place it. Space. Elbow room. Freedom?

His mind cut off the thought before it had a chance to germinate and put down roots. He had already blown his chance, and had been punished for the effort. Chong had taken pleasure in the ceremony, held the knife himself and brought it down, with the other P.O.W.'s looking on. It was a lesson, not so much to Bradford, but to any others who might try to follow his example.

It would have been just as easy for Chong to kill him, but that would have been a mercy, a reward, and Chong was far too clever to be duped so easily. He knew his prisoners, their terrors and weaknesses. He knew how far he could push each one of them, how much their weakened bodies could endure before he lost them.

Chong was a professional at inflicting suffering, and he seemed to love his work. Bradford wished he could have a chance to kill the camp commander, but he knew that was impossible, a dream he cherished in the silent darkness of the night.

But still, there was something . . . something *different* in his environment. He had fallen, he could feel familiar earth against his cheek, but there was no room in his cage to stand and fall. If that was true . . .

He was outside! The hand upon his arm, the slide across the threshold of his cell—these had not been dreamed, imagined.

He was out!

Bradford rolled over onto his stomach, fighting desperately to focus on the sounds of combat all around him. Automatic weapons, bullets striking earth and splintering bamboo. A battle, close at hand, almost surrounding him.

He opened bleary eyes and saw a figure clad in camouflage fatigues, crouching just in front of him, firing in the general direction of Chong's command hut with an assault rifle. From the man's size, Bradford knew he was a Westerner, but the outfit and gear told him nothing more.

Another figure leaped into his field of vision, and there could be no mistaking this one. It was Mandrell, still decked out in his faded, jungle-rotted uniform, and he was carrying an AK-47, laying down a stream of fire from one end of the nearest barracks to the other. He was dancing, stroking out short bursts and interspersing them with longer ones whenever a moving target presented itself. He seemed to be having the time of his life.

Realization struck Alex Bradford like a fist above the heart, and as he recognized his situation and knew that it might last only another moment, or maybe forever, he brought his legs up beneath him with a supreme effort, using his remaining hand and the stump of his left wrist to push himself upward, rising to his feet.

A bullet buzzed beside his ear, and Bradford flinched away from it, grinning fiercely in spite of himself. He knew what Mandrell was feeling, could feel something of the grim, suicidal elation himself.

Someone had come for them, goddammit, and it didn't matter who or why, it no longer counted even if the rescue attempt was unsuccessful. All that mattered was the effort, and Bradford knew that he would die, standing up and fighting back, barehanded if need be, before he let Chong put him back inside a cage.

He cast about for something, anything, with which to join the battle. Twenty yards away and to his left, a sentry sprawled facedown beside the fire, his automatic rifle inches from one outstretched hand. Bradford focused on the weapon, forgetting everything else in that supreme moment of concentration, putting one rubbery leg in front of the other and reeling away from the cages like a drunkard.

He covered all of seven strides before gravity overcame his weakened muscles and pulled him down. The hard earth rushed to meet him, the impact knocked the breath out of him, and then the sounds of firing carried him away.

Terrance Loughlin squeezed another burst out of his overheated assault carbine, then set the smoking gun aside. He reached down for the detonator on the ground beside him, found it without ever taking his eyes off the killing ground in front of him.

The Britisher had made good use of his time in preparation for the raid. While Stone and Hog were staking out the village, counting sentries and determining their beats, he had performed a penetration of his own upon the enemy encampment. Nothing deep, no contact, strictly silent ...

but he was about to make his presence felt among the Vietnamese in a way that they would not forget. Assuming that they lived.

He had selected certain buildings in the compound for disposal, and gooped them with generous helpings of his C-4 plastic explosive, plugging in the detonators that would let him set them off, simultaneously or in sequence, with a touch on the buttons of his radio remote-control box. Moving swiftly, silently, taking care to miss the roving sentries, he had mined the communications hut, the generator shack, and several of the long, low barracks buildings. Time restrictions had prevented him from dropping off a package at the camp command post, but from what he could see, the occupants had problems enough at the moment.

As for the rest...

He raised the detonator box, found the first of several deadly buttons with his index finger, and pressed it lightly. On his left front, the communications shack seemed to rise on a plume of fire, the four walls blowing outward simultaneously, thatched roof disintegrating into flaming strands of grass. Personnel, equipment, everything inside was gone within the twinkling of an eye.

Smiling, Loughlin stroked the second button, then the third. Two barracks huts went up almost together, like twin giant firecrackers on the southern perimeter of the camp. Parts of bodies were airborne now, raining down on the camp like fallout from an exploding butcher shop. Twenty feet away, a human arm fell to the earth, still smoking, fingers clenched in death.

The commando let his other charges go in tandem, throwing a ring of blazing death around the camp, bringing down the fires of hell upon his enemies. The charges wouldn't get them all, or even most of them, but they would damn sure add confusion to the recipe, and that was all he asked for at the moment.

Chaos was an ally tonight, helping to buy the time they needed for delivery of their human quarry from the cages in the center of the camp. Stone was there already, busy at the task and taking fire while he was at it. Loughlin moved to help his comrade, breaking out of cover with the CAR-15 at his hip and roaring as he joined the dance of death.

They had to stand together now, fight their way out as a unit, or they would be cut off and slaughtered piecemeal.

Loughlin kept his head down, running in a combat crouch, the stream of bullets from his automatic rifle opening the way and leaving twisted, writhing bodies in his wake. Another thirty yards and he would make it. After that, they only had to stand off an army, and fight their way back through the living jungle to their transportation rendezvous. Simple. It would be as easy as falling off a log—and landing in an empty, open grave.

Mark Stone was fighting for his life, and for the moment he was not sure who was winning. Enemies were all around him, pouring constant fire into his position, and the ring of bamboo cages offered precious little in the way of fortification. He had spent two magazines already, and beside him, crouching under cover and returning bursts each time the ground fire lifted, Jack Mandrell was clearly low on ammunition.

In the end, it was the Britisher who saved them with his plastic charges. At once, half of the enemy forces were thrown into confusion, firing now in all directions, certain that hostile reinforcements were assailing them on every side.

Stone paused, correcting himself.

On every side but one.

Loughlin had been careful in his planting of the charges, leaving them an avenue of exit to the west. While the explosives danced and flared around them, tossing men and equipment skyward like toys, the westward way lay open, virtually unguarded. Just a scattering of fire from that direction, but Stone knew that they could make it—if the others kept their heads and made it in on schedule.

As if in answer to his thought, he spotted Loughlin weaving through the chaos, dodging bullets, bodies, and shrapnel. A wounded sentry blundered out into his path, and Loughlin felled him with a buttstroke from his carbine, scattering the guy's dentition on the ground like so many Chiclets.

He made it, sliding in on one side, winging a short burst back along his track and taking out a tail that hung a bit too close for comfort. He was grinning as he turned to face Stone, but the smile was gone the instant he took in the P.O.W.'s.

The Britisher's eyes lingered painfully over Alex Bradford, missing nothing, and he cursed beneath his breath.

"Bloody bastards."

Stone clapped him on the shoulder.

"Bloodier now than they were before you set those charges off. It's working like a charm."

"We aim to please. Where's Hog?"

"Right here!"

The big man barreled in on top of them, rolling across the top of a bullet-splintered bamboo cage and almost collapsing it beneath his bulk. Lan Vang was right behind him, and Stone did a rapid head count, reassuring himself in an instant that everyone was present and accounted for, ready to attempt the break. They would have to get it right the first time. There would be no second chance.

He jabbed an index finger at Bradford's prostrate form.

"This one can't make it on his own," he snapped. "We'll have to haul him out."

"No sweat."

Before he'd finished speaking, Hog Wiley had the unconscious P.O.W. draped across one meaty shoulder in a fireman's carry. Somehow he even managed to leave both hands free for his CAR-15.

The other P.O.W.'s were watching Stone, taking in his every word of explanation, nodding in unison as they agreed to follow him unquestioningly, obeying every order on the instant. If they failed, each of them knew that death would be a blessing in comparison to their recapture by the enemy.

"Okay. On me!" Stone barked, and he was moving now, before the echoes of Loughlin's explosions had died away in the jungle night. Firing as he ran, and moving toward the gap they had blasted in the line, he trusted that the others were behind him, following his lead as he had ordered. From here on, each man was on his own, and there would be no time to rescue stragglers.

They were sprinting out of hell and straight into the open dragon's mouth. Taking the war to the enemy, and ramming every cold-steel inch of it right down his bloody, gaping throat.

Captain Chong picked himself up from where the force of the exploding communications hut deposited him. Dazed, the camp commandant did not reflect on his luck at sustaining only a cut along his forehead, but fought to control his troops, to salvage something from what had the making's of a catastrophe. By now he knew the prisoners were gone, somehow abducted by the hostile force. He also knew that if he did not get them back at once, he would not have to worry about being stationed out here in the middle of the jungle.

He would not be stationed anywhere again. Ever.

His superiors would not permit a captain who lost prisoners to risk disgracing them a second time. Chong knew that he would simply disappear without a trace, and that would be the end of everything—his plans, his dreams of wealth and power in the new regime.

Chong stiffened, swallowing the lump of fear that had been growing in his throat. He was not beaten yet. There were still ways of redeeming the situation, perhaps even turning it to his advantage. But first he had to win back the control over his men which would be necessary to his plan.

Drawing his automatic pistol from its holster, Chong strode out into the middle of the campsite battlefield, shouting and cursing, firing his weapon into earth and air as he tried to get the attention of his panicked men. At first the shooting only seemed to merge with the general chaos reigning over the camp, but gradually, as some of the troops recognized him, the firing slacked away, and finally died out altogether.

He marshaled them with shouts and curses, slapping and kicking those who moved too slowly for his pleasure. They were slowly beaten into ranks, given moments to reload while he berated them, denouncing them all as cowards, unworthy of the uniforms they wore. They were disgraced, finished in the service, condemned to death or prison for permitting the American dogs to escape so easily.

Unless they helped him win the P.O.W.'s back, of course, and punish the guerrillas who had taken them in the first place.

He could see a glimmer of hope behind the sullen eyes, growing here and there until the men were straining toward him, eager to be off on the chase. He held them back now, deliberately, wasting precious time and giving the enemy a few more yards head start while he whipped his troops' anger and hatred to a fever pitch.

Each man among them knew that his own life was riding on the outcome of the chase. And what they might not care to do for Captain Chong, each one of them would do, and more, to save himself.

At last he let them go, bringing up the rear as the point

men led out. They would not pause to rest until the enemy was taken.

Chong was pleased—but still not confident. The enemy and his prisoners were still out there somewhere ahead of him, moving through the darkness of the forest at top speed, perhaps already making for some rendezvous with vehicles prepared to carry them away to safety.

If they escaped...

He put the thought away from him, refusing to consider it. He would not, *could not* fail. Instead, he would emerge victorious: the camp commander who had withstood a full assault by hostile troops on friendly ground, then recouped his losses by retaining his prisoners and killing or capturing the entire enemy force.

He smiled at the darkness, keeping pace with the column of his troops now, adrenaline pumping through his body. He would succeed where other, lesser men would surely fail. It was his destiny, and he was bound for greater things.

Chapter Seventeen

Stone saw the liana coming just in time to duck it, hunching down and moving on without a break in stride. The jungle after nightfall was an obstacle course where any misstep might prove fatal to unwary travelers. A different sort of predator enjoyed the night: lethal reptiles and insects, prowling in an endless search for food.

There was no time for caution now, not with the armed pursuit force inevitably on their trail. Stone knew that the Viets would not be far behind them. The commander of the camp, or his subordinates if he had fallen in the firefight, would be anxious to redeem themselves, recoup their losses. They would keep up with the chase all night, if necessary, right on to the border, in their hatred and their hunger for revenge.

Stone knew that he had just deprived the camp commander and his men of their precious self-respect. They must avenge themselves, or die in the attempt; their honor would not let them go back to their own superiors and readily confess defeat by any smaller force.

Surprise had been the key, and Stone knew that his enemies would still be reeling, even as they took up the pursuit. They could not know, for certain, just how many men had participated in the raid. Their fear of contact with a larger force, determined, better armed, would slow their steps a little—perhaps enough to give Stone's column all the lead they needed to effect their getaway.

Perhaps.

But he certainly couldn't count on it with any confidence.

His years of jungle warfare had taught Stone one thing above all else: a man always had to be prepared, expect the unexpected. It was trite, a virtual cliché, but that did not deprive the maxim of its basic truthfulness.

The jungle was not enemy or friend, he knew. The landscape, animals, and vegetation were indifferent to the schemes of men, uninterested in the war games they played across the land. From experience, he knew the jungle to be neutral—and that made it every bit as dangerous as any foe. The jungle didn't give a damn who won this war or that one; it devoured friends and enemies with fine impartiality, consuming everyone and everything that had the temerity to trespass in its vast domain.

Stone did not fear the jungle. He respected it. And tonight he knew that it could work either for him or against him as he raced the clock, determined to keep their rendezvous with the waiting helicopter.

It would be close, no doubt about it. They were running behind schedule now, and they would have to make it up along the way unless they wanted to wind up walking back to Bangkok. It was possible, of course, but Stone was sure his charges would not survive the trek. Alex Bradford would almost certainly die along the way, unless he got some medical attention soon.

Lan Vang was leading them along what seemed to be a narrow game trail, carved out of the forest by millennia of paws and hooves intent on finding food and water. With any luck at all, it would lead them to their rendezvous, and they would get there intact before the pilot started getting edgy in the predawn darkness, and decided to take off without them.

Stone tried to picture Meyers and Hopkins waiting in the Huey, narrowed eyes probing and dissecting the hostile darkness. They would wait for the allotted span of time because he owed them cash, if for no other reason. But he could not count on anything if they were late in keeping the appointment. Meyers and Hopkins might hang in a little longer—or they might take off and leave the little column to its fate.

Either way, time was of the essence, and the more so if they missed connections with the Huey. If they had to hike out through the jungle, they would need every moment of lead time they could get, to keep ahead of the pursuing enemy.

A sound of rushing, hissing water, and before he knew it, Stone was standing on a riverbank. A second glance told him it was really more a stream than a real river, but it was swift, and looked pretty deep out there, toward the center, where the water swirled and eddied.

They would have to cross, and there was no time for rigging any sort of grabline. They were going to get wet, and there was nothing he could do about it now, except to curse the darkness and the water that had blocked their path.

Lan Vang was first down in the stream, and he was waist-deep before he had taken five strides out from the bank. The current sucked around and at his legs, almost toppling him twice before he made it to midstream. Stone watched him closely, trying to calculate the depth of the water, using the Laotian's diminutive height as a gauge.

Hog Wiley brushed against him in the darkness of the jungle, still carrying Colonel Bradford slung across his shoulders.

"Can you carry him across?" Stone asked.

Hog eyed the water dubiously, and finally nodded.

"Shouldn't be a problem. Poor bastard hardly weighs a hundred pounds."

"All right. You take the lead, and I'll be right behind you, just in case."

"Roger that."

Without a backward glance, the towering Hog started wading out into the rushing stream, his human cargo high and dry. Stone cast a backward glance at Terrance Loughlin, knowing he would watch the ambulatory P.O.W.'s and protect them on the crossing as best he could.

The water was surprisingly warm on Stone's legs and buttocks as he left the bank and waded out toward mid-stream. He tried to follow Hog as closely as he could, careful to test each step before he committed himself, putting his full weight down only when the bottom of the stream proved to be solid, able to support him. There were stones along the bottom, shifting in the ooze, and it reminded Stone of trying to walk on marbles that some child had scattered thoughtlessly about.

No time to worry now about what forms of jungle life might be sharing the river with them. Rushing water pretty well ruled out the usual leeches and other denizens of stagnant ponds. There might well be snakes, of course, and the ever-present crocodiles, but Stone would not allow himself to dwell on them, would not permit his mind to call up the image of the Vietnamese patrol boat sailor, going down amid the swirl of bloody water lashed to lather by a broad reptilian tail.

He had enough to worry about, enough to fear this night from men. No need to borrow trouble from Mother Nature.

They were something more than halfway across the stream when Hog lost his footing, gave a stifled little groan, and tumbled over sideways. He kept his grip on Alex Bradford's legs, but the current of the stream was sucking at them both, threatening to drag him under, or deprive him of his human burden.

Stone started splashing toward them at the double. Reaching down, he tangled his fingers in the wounded colonel's hair and yanked his face above the surface of the water. Bradford gave a long, shuddering gasp, expelling water from his nose and mouth, and then Hog was scrambling to his feet, cursing fluently as he regained his balance and his grip upon the wounded prisoner.

"Okay?" Stone asked above the sound of the rushing water.

"Got 'im," Hog grunted, already turning back and moving on toward the opposite bank.

Stone risked a backward glance and saw Loughlin and the others crossing without apparent incident, closing the gap between them. He continued on, and gained the bank a moment after Wiley made it, gratefully depositing his bundle on the mossy bank and dropping to a restful crouch.

"No time for that," Stone told him, motioning to Lan Vang to hit the trail again as soon as Loughlin and his charges reached the bank and scrambled dripping from the water. "We can rest on board the Huey."

"Shit."

Hog hauled himself erect without another word, hoisted Alex Bradford on his meaty shoulders, and moved out to follow without further protest.

All of them were well aware of what recapture would mean for the P.O.W.'s—and what it would mean for Stone's group if the Vietnamese were able to take them alive. Stone had survived captivity in Asian hands himself, and he had no desire whatever to repeat the lesson.

He would not be taken alive, no matter the outcome of their race with time. If it came down to that, he chose a death in combat, standing up and facing down the enemy, hand-to-hand and eye-to-eye. A soldier's death, rather than the rotting, living hell of some crude zoo in the highlands.

As for the others, they had talked it over many times, before and after missions like the present one, and Stone knew they were in accord. Surrender was as foreign to these men as fear, no part of their vocabulary. While they might retreat, it was strategic, never coming close to the rout they had inflicted on defenders at the prison camp so very recently.

Their mission was accomplished, so they left.

Stone paused, mentally correcting himself. Their mission was *almost* accomplished. There was still the trifling matter of an exit out of Laos, and safe delivery of their charges to their waiting families.

Mandrell and Wilcox were the wild cards. Mark Stone had come in search of only one P.O.W., Alex Bradford, and now he was going home with three. He had no idea whether there was family waiting for the other two or not. Most likely, they had long been given up for dead. Sometimes the wives remarried or found other solace, and the children, some of them no more than infants when their fathers had gone to war, could hardly be expected to remember from a picture on the mantel.

It was rough, no doubt about it, but the men behind him deserved another shot at life, no matter what that life turned out to be. If they were forced to uproot certain memories and find an opening for others, it was better, sure as hell, than rotting in a bamboo cage in Laos.

No P.O.W. in Stone's experience had ever shown regret at leaving his captivity, and these were no exception. As they traveled, covering the ground and clicking off kilometers in darkness, even Wilcox seemed more animated, more coherent than the zombie that Stone had first encountered on his initial penetration of the camp. Not speaking, well aware of all security precautions, Wilcox still seemed more alert and awake, and he was keeping in close touch with his cellmate, Mandrell, through a system of grunts and hand signals they had obviously worked out through the years of their captivity.

Stone left them to it, and he didn't give a damn if they were cutting paper dolls back there, as long as they could stand the pace, and not hold the column back. So far, he was pleasantly surprised by the stamina of the two ambulatory prisoners; he had expected them to be so weakened and emaciated that all three would have to be carried the majority of the way.

Stone heard the sounds an instant before Lan Vang froze in his tracks, a dozen yards ahead of the advancing column. They were sounds of battle—with a difference. Between the shouts and jungle-muffled sounds of sporadic gunfire, there was something else: a noise like raucous, throaty laughter.

Stone raised a hand, signaling the others to wait where they were with their charges. He moved up beside their Free Laotian guide, and together the two of them slipped through the undergrowth, homing on the source of the sounds ahead. A gliding, slow advance of fifty yards, and there was nothing in the least bit muffled about the sounds now.

A woman screamed, and Stone could hear the sound of knuckles striking flesh as she was quickly silenced. Another burst of gunshots, almost casual, followed by another strangled scream.

Stone reached out cautiously to part the ferns in front of him, allowing himself to view the battlefield beyond. There was a little village up ahead, carved out of a jungle clearing, temporary, judging from the makeshift huts and hastily constructed cooking fire. The villagers, perhaps a score of peasants dressed in ragged garb, were herded close together by the fire, surrounded by a motley force of well-armed men.

Two of the men were occupied in attempting to drag a fighting and kicking young woman into the nearest thatched hut. Her jacket had been torn away already to reveal her teenaged breasts, and she was fighting the inevitable with grim tenacity.

"What's going on?" he asked their guide, although Stone thought he knew the answer independently.

Lan Vang spent another moment surveying the scene, and then leaned closer, his narrow lips almost brushing Stone's ear as he whispered his answer.

"Bandits!"

Chapter Eighteen

Stone watched the action for another moment, easing off the safety on his rifle. He was weighing angles, calculating probabilities, assessing needs. The villagers were clearly in the worst of trouble, but his men, especially the P.O.W.'s, were in equal jeopardy, or worse. Delay to intervene in what was not his fight would give Stone's enemies a chance to cut their lead, to close the gap and come in striking distance. Worse, it ran the risk of making them impossibly late for the rendezvous with Meyers and the Huey.

And Stone already knew the answer to the silent question he had asked himself. Before he started running down the reasons for remaining uninvolved, he knew that he could not stay out of this one.

Because it *was* his fight, from the beginning. When a man took up arms against the savages, there could be no fine dividing lines between the enemies he chose. And if he passed these helpless victims by, he would be worse than those who tormented them originally.

There was something deep inside Mark Stone that would not let him walk away from this one, not while there were lives in danger in the tiny village.

He worked his way back to the others, briefed them on the action up ahead, let them have their own say, voice opinions that differed from his own. But there were no dissenters. Even Jack Mandrell seemed happy, almost eager, to engage the enemy on any front at all, as long as he was doing something, being part of it.

Stone moved along the narrow game trail, swiftly joined Lan Vang again, and nodded confirmation of his plan. They would go straight ahead, right through the village, on their way to the helicopter rendezvous, and if the bandits tried to stop them...

Well, there was nothing they could do about it, except to fight their way through, level their enemies as they presented themselves for execution.

Stone started counting down to the jump-off, waiting for the others to take their posts in the early-morning darkness. When he heard and felt them at their stations, he was ready, anxious now to get his feet wet, have it over and done with.

In the center of the little village, the bandits were herding unarmed civilians together, grouping them as if for one last collective photograph. But those were automatic weapons they were leveling at the tiny crowd, not cameras, and another moment would see the massacre completed, whether Stone stepped in or not.

Stone raised his own CAR-15, sighting on the nearest bandit, and squeezed off a burst as he exploded from his jungle cover. All around him, weapons opened up along the line of fire, announcing the arrival of the cavalry.

They still might be too late, might rue the day they crossed the bandits' path, but they were in it now, and there was no way out except the other side, dead or free and clear. Mark Stone would not have had it any other way.

Hog Wiley leveled two of the slender bandits with a single burst from his carbine, and watched the clutch of villagers disintegrate, the members streaking off in all directions like so much human shrapnel. He was dodging, weaving, firing at the human targets as they were presented to him, ducking bullets as they reached for him, tugging at his clothing in the darkness.

He felt the enemy approaching from his flank, silently, without a warning sound of any kind. Hog spun to face him, leveling the rifle, squeezing off—and cursing as the slide locked open on an empty chamber.

The bandit was upon him, handgun raised and tracking on his face. Reacting swiftly, Wiley brought the wooden stock of his weapon up and over, smashing into the bandit's gun hand and knocking the pistol spinning, flashing off in the direction of the central cookfire.

Hog followed up the first advantage of surprise, clubbing his opponent with the rifle stock, smashing cheek and jaw, altering the gunner's face so that even his own mother wouldn't recognize him. Blood and teeth went flying, and on the second stroke, an eyeball was ejected from its socket, swinging on the optic nerve and tattered muscles like a tiny tetherball.

The guy was blinded, reeling in his agony, and Hog finished him with a one-two combination, his combat boots smashing up and into his groin, the rifle stock whipping around and down to meet the crown of his skull as the pain below collapsed him.

Hog left him on the hard-packed earth of the clearing, and moved on in search of other enemies. He reloaded his rifle on the run, discarding the empty magazine and slamming another into the receiver as he circled warily around the fire. Stepping across a civilian, he neared the closest hut—and was surprised by the explosive exit of a battered, naked female. Close behind her raced a bandit, hobbled by the pants that had fallen around his ankles, his manhood erect and bobbing in the breeze.

Hog swung the rifle stock around and hit the fleshy nail right on the head, driving it backward an inch and stopping its owner dead in his tracks. The gunner's mouth fell open, and a strangled little cry emerged before Hog plugged that sewer with the muzzle of his AK-47, squeezing off a two-round burst that took the head and everything above his Adam's apple, and put the whole mess into orbit.

Another rifleman was having second thoughts about emerging from the hut, and Wiley helped him make the grim decision, ripping off a burst that cut his legs from under him and deposited him screaming on the doorstep. A combat boot crashed down with crushing force upon the juncture of his skull and spine, and he was silent, still.

Hog Wiley moved away from there, still hunting. There was something in Hog's blood that called for killing now, a fever, a primordial fury, as he witnessed what these human animals had done to helpless villagers. He was a giant avenging angel, cut from no usual angelic pattern, granted, but avenging them in any case, whether or not they recognized salvation when they saw it. The din of battle filled his ears, almost aphrodisiac in its intensity, and he was grinning as he sought the suddenly reluctant enemy in every nook and cranny of the little village, hunting.

Terrance Loughlin crouched and waited as the rifleman came rushing toward him, leveling the bayonet and giving a high, unearthly scream. When he was less than twenty feet away, the Britisher let him have a burst, stitching him from groin to throat and opening him like a sack of grain, depositing his entrails on the ground before the body proper made its touchdown.

Moving on into the battle smoke, he watched the others on his flanks, Stone and Wiley, Lan Vang and the P.O.W., Jack Mandrell. It would be easy to pick off a brother by mistake, and such mistakes were costly. A careful soldier lived to fight another day, and Loughlin had survived this long by being careful to the max.

And still, when death came calling for him, he was almost taken unaware. He heard the rush, felt the disturbance of the air on his immediate right—and then the blade of a machete whistled past his face, missing the tip of his nose by a fraction of an inch, ringing off the receiver of his CAR-15.

The blow was stunning, setting up vibrations in his hands and forearms, knocking the autorifle from his grasp and dashing it to earth.

He sprang back, knowing there would be no time to retrieve the assault rifle, clawing at the .45 upon his hip. The machete-wielding bandit was upon him in a split second, shouting, swinging his broad-bladed chopper like a madman, advancing steadily and driving Loughlin back in the direction of the jungle.

Terrance had the automatic, and was about to draw it and relieve himself of this opponent, when the bandit rushed him, shrieking his hatred in a reedy, high-pitched voice. The blade was whistling down directly toward his face, and Loughlin went in low, inside the swing, closing the gap instead of retreating, realizing that it was his only chance.

He took the blow upon an upraised forearm, coming in beneath the swing, letting the machete whistle past above his head, cleaving empty air, as he blocked the killer's arm. At the same time, the stiffened fingers of his own right hand were stabbing upward, searching for the gunner's solar plexus, finding it and probing deep with lightning speed, knocking the wind out of him, doubling him over.

A roundhouse kick brought the heel of Loughlin's boot against the gasping bandit's skull and drove him sideways, reeling in the open clearing. Loughlin followed through, already reaching for the useless, dangling knife arm, locking on the wrist and twisting, putting weight and leverage behind it, feeling bones as they began to grate together, twisting, snapping audibly.

The bandit screamed, released his death grip on the long machete, and let it fall. Loughlin retrieved it in a second, brought it up and over in a two-handed swing, the razor-edged blade impacting on the nape of its owner's neck at full speed and strength.

The bandit's head appeared to hang there for a moment, suspended in midair, and then it bounced away, leaving the decapitated body standing on its own before gravity reasserted itself and pulled it down. Loughlin wasted no time with the dead, already moving back to pick up his rifle before the next attacker found him. He could not count on luck to see him through this one; a soldier made the breaks with what he had available, and Terrance Loughlin was an old hand at survival.

He would survive this one, as well, but other lives would pay the price. He planned to see that all those lives were hostile ones, the dead men only enemies.

Jack Mandrell was smiling as he stroked the trigger of his captured rifle, ripping another automatic burst into the ranks of the retreating bandits, watching as they toppled, spinning, sprawling on the blood-drenched earth. Two of them down, and three. Another, just emerging from a hut upon his right, still zipping up his pants and smiling at the memory of stolen sex, and Mandrell blew him back into the darkened doorway.

It was good to fight, to kill.

The accumulated rage of years was high inside him now, and flowing through the muzzle of his borrowed weapon, streaking through the night on steel-jacketed wings.

He was a man again, and there was nothing that the damned Vietnamese could do to rob him of the feeling that that knowledge gave him. They could kill him, and they probably would, but he would die contented now that he had seen the opportunity to pay them back in kind, to let them feel the pain and fear of death with nowhere left to hide.

It didn't matter now what happened to him; life or death, escape or capture, it was all the same to Jack Mandrell. He had seen his chance, seized it with both hands and run with it as far as human strength could take him. He had done his best, enjoyed his freedom for a few hours, and if it all fell apart in the next minute, he would have nothing to regret . . . except perhaps that he had not enjoyed the thrill of meeting Captain Chong and squeezing off a magazine between those hated, sloping eyes.

That would have been a victory, and something to remember as his life was flashing before his eyes, but as it was . . .

Mandrell's rifle emptied out in a roaring, bucking burst, and he ditched the empty magazine and snapped a replacement into the receiver. He was running low, no doubt about it, but it didn't matter. If he got the chance, he could retrieve more ammunition from the fallen bandits all around him. If he didn't—well, who gave a damn?

And suddenly he realized that one thing mattered to him, after all. The vision of recapture, of submitting to Chong's rule and punishments again, rose up to haunt him like a nightmare specter, guiding his hand and his hatred as he spied another bandit and sent him sprawling with a well-timed burst of automatic fire.

Jack Mandrell knew that he would never surrender, never allow himself to be held captive in a cage again. Even if he had to die. Even if he had to kill himself.

It was too much to ask of any man, and he would not return to that—whatever might befall him here tonight.

Jack Mandrell had found his freedom, and if necessary he would take it with him to the grave. But he would die a man, standing on his own two feet and fighting back, dishing out some hell to the enemies who had imprisoned him and shamed him through the years, instead of giving up and crawling back to them on hands and knees.

He would live free or die, damned right, and there was no real choice, from where he stood. Freedom was life, and life was freedom. There would be no more of that zombie-like existence in the camps. Mandrell had spent his time in purgatory, and now he was blasting out, and God help anyone or anything who tried to bar his way.

Chapter Nineteen

The sounds of battle were winding down by slow degrees, the rattle of automatic fire becoming more sporadic, less a constant background music for the dance of death. The enemies were few and far between now, scattered fugitives more intent upon escape with skins intact than with continuing the fight or seeking revenge.

Stone ducked through the doorway of a small thatched hut, pursuing the sound of a muffled, sobbing scream that reached his ears above the heavy-metal sounds of combat. Moving swiftly to one side, refusing to be silhouetted in the doorway, he swept the semidark interior with his CAR-15, freezing the three occupants in a little tableau.

And it was no nativity scene that met his eyes, but something dark, primeval. Stone took in the elderly couple huddled in the corner, their open throats smiling back at him in the half-light, drooling crimson. Flat, dead eyes regarded his arrival with the ultimate disinterest. Stone had come too late for them, and they no longer had the time to wait for him.

The others, centered in the dingy little room, were still alive—for the moment.

Stone counted two of the bandits. Crouched down between them, sobbing, was the woman he had seen at the beginning of the battle. She was naked now, her face streaked with tears and blood that coursed from scalp wounds where the men had beaten her to force submission. Other cuts and welts were evident upon her body, covering her breasts and belly in an ugly tic-tac-toe of agony.

The bandits faced him, one of them offering a sickly smile and giggling, as if in hope that some fraternity could pass between them. He was reaching for a brotherhood that Stone had never been a part of, seeking for some sympathy from one defiler of women to another—and he had most emphatically come to the wrong place this time.

Stone smiled right back at him—and shot the outlaw's comrade first, his bullets slamming into the gunner's groin, emasculating him before they made the spiral climb through guts and ribcage to kill him on his feet, before he hit the ground.

The grinning idiot saw what was coming now, and he was trying every other tack he knew, from tears to jabbered pleas, abruptly kneeling as the automatic rifle tracked in his direction.

Stone left him to it for perhaps three heartbeats, then he blew the bandit's slimy ass away and watched him come apart beneath the stream of manglers, jerking back and forth like a marionette in the hands of some spastic puppeteer.

Stone let the clip empty out and then reloaded swiftly, in a single fluid motion, as he left the hut. There was no way for him to offer consolation to the woman, no more time for lingering in that house of death. She would do what she must, and he had done the only thing he could to help her. It was in larger, universal hands, and out of his.

Outside, the night was silent now, except for whispered voices that Stone recognized immediately. Hog and Lough-lin, calling to each other on the killing ground, Lan Vang responding from his little corner of the war. And then Man-drell, the P.O.W., rounded the corner of a nearby hut, rifle slung across one shoulder at a jaunty angle, smiling like a boy out on his first hunt of the season.

They regrouped around the cookfire, taking stock of their situation, and Wiley retrieved the other P.O.W.'s from their cover in the bush. All the bandits were accounted for, and if any of them escaped, that was all right with Stone. They would still be running this time tomorrow, no thought of coming back with reinforcements. There would be no more danger from that quarter, certainly, but they were far from out of trouble yet.

It took another lengthy moment for the villagers to start returning, filtering back from the jungle darkness, taking no chances as they cautiously approached the strangers who had saved them from the outlaws. They were wary, never knowing whether their saviors of the moment might become their new tormentors, but in time they grouped together, drawing closer, one old man moving forward to address the little clutch of armed commandos.

"I am Tran Binh," he announced. "I am the headman of this village."

Stone nodded a greeting, wishing he would get to the point and let them go.

"You have done us a service, preserved us from this filth. We owe you much."

"Forget it," Stone replied. "The scum were in our way. We removed them."

"As you say, but there are debts which we cannot repay, except in kind. A warning. You are all in danger, even as we speak."

Stone frowned, and Wiley cracked, "The old bird's psychic."

"Danger? What danger do you speak of?" Stone inquired.

The head man pointed to westward, in the general direction of their march.

"The Pathet Lao are coming," he explained. "A large patrol was seen by one of our scouts earlier this evening. They are coming this way, rounding up refugees, hunting for guerrillas in the forest."

He paused before continuing, sweeping Stone and the others with narrowed, knowing eyes, taking in their stock of weapons and their military uniforms.

"We were about to break camp and leave, when the bandits surprised us. It was my fault. I forgot to post a sentry in my haste to get away."

"Forget about it," Stone advised him. "Everybody makes mistakes, and you survived this one. When will the Pathet Lao arrive?"

"Soon. I cannot say with certainty, but they were three or four hours out when we were warned. Almost three hours ago."

Stone cursed, and Wiley seconded it. They were running out of time, behind their schedule now, with the Vietnamese upon their track and doubtless closing fast. If there was anything they didn't need precisely at that moment, it was other enemies approaching from the west, cutting off their avenue of retreat, their line of exit to the chopper rendezvous and home.

They didn't need it, but now they had it, all the same.

Mark Stone was thinking rapidly, weighing the alternatives. They could strike off at an oblique angle, cutting a detour through the forest, but the time that they would lose, even supposing that they met no flankers from the Pathet Lao patrol, would put them hours behind their already failing schedule. If they blundered straight ahead, unmindful of the threat, they ran the risk of confronting a superior enemy force in the dark, on unfamiliar ground. They could easily be wiped out before they knew what hit them.

And that brought him to the one alternative that seemed to offer any hope of success: to stay in place, wait out the storm, and hope the Pathet Lao were every bit as prompt as the headman seemed to indicate.

There were some risks inherent in the plan, of course, and Stone was not discounting them. The village was not built for armed defense; the earlier experience with the bandits made that point with crystal clarity. At the same time, any further delay, let alone a holding action in the middle of the jungle, put them that much farther behind their rigid schedule.

It was touch-and-go, but there was nothing else to do. They would dig in, prepare to fight, and if the Vietnamese trackers overtook them in the meantime...

Stone smiled to himself as another plan, more refined and detailed, more sophisticated, came to mind.

There just might be a way to kill two vultures with a single stone, if he was quick enough. And if the shaken, frightened villagers would help him with the plan that he was formulating.

"We will wait for them here," he said at last, seeing the surprise on the headman's face, and on the faces of his own armed men, as well.

Hog was looking at him like someone who sees a friend begin to dance the funky chicken at an embassy reception, and the Britisher was shaking his head in grim bewilderment. As for the P.O.W.'s, two of them were seemingly oblivious to what was going on around them, lost in a delirious world of their own, and Jack Mandrell was smiling at him and nodding as if he relished the idea of another armed engagement with the hostiles.

Stone frowned and turned away from the recent captive's

scrutiny. He wondered if his plan was really so insane that only madmen could see what he had in mind and yield to his suggestion.

Never mind. It was the only choice available, and that made it no goddamned choice at all. They were bound to die if they left the village on a blind rush fore or aft, and wandering away to north or south would simply lose them in the jungle, cost them days of doubling back, provided they had the time to start with.

He would stand and fight, because it was the only thing to do. And his associates would stand beside him in his choice, because they trusted him—because, in the final analysis, they either stood or fell together. There was nowhere for the rest of them to go alone.

He started speaking rapidly, outlining what he wanted his men and the villagers to do, the role that they would play in the engagement he was planning. They were listening, nodding in agreement, grudgingly at first, and then with more enthusiasm as the scheme revealed itself. By the time he finished speaking, he could tell that they were with him, still uncertain of the outcome, naturally, but willing to see it through and find out if it had a chance of working.

If it worked, they all could walk away from this intact, perhaps with time to keep their LZ rendezvous.

And if it failed, then Meyers could take off without them, holding to his schedule, and pocket the retainer for his pains.

The money would be meaningless to Stone and company if this last desperate plan fell through. For cash meant nothing to a dead man, and there were no bars or cathouses in hell.

Stone put the grim, defeatist line of thought away from him and started concentrating on the fine points of his plan. There were things to be done, orders to be issued, preparations to be finalized before the Vietnamese and Pathet Lao moved in to take them by surprise.

Mark Stone was counting on a little surprise of his own this evening, looking forward to the effect his scheme would have upon the enemy if it worked smoothly. If it failed . . . well, then, he wouldn't have to bear the shame for long.

Dead men never felt embarrassment.

Chapter Twenty

It was doubly dark inside the hut, a combination of the velvet night outside and the enclosure of the walls surrounding him. The dual effect was almost crushingly oppressive. Mark Stone kept his eye upon the gun slit he had cut an inch above the hard-packed earthen floor . . . and waited.

They had passed an anxious hour since completing the fortifications of their makeshift village stronghold. Time was dragging now, each moment ticking off their chances of making the chopper rendezvous on time and with their human cargo intact. As it was, they would be hard-pressed now to keep their crucial appointment, even if they left immediately.

But they had to wait. The time elapsed had not deprived them of all choices in the matter. From the moment they had agreed to stand and make a fight of it, the little warrior band was out of options, locked into the game of life and death.

The only question now was which of their enemies would arrive first. It mattered little, but Mark Stone was counting on the timing to assist him in his plan. It did not have to be precise—the jungle and the darkness would allow for some margin of error—but it had damned well better be *close,* or they were all in for trouble of the terminal variety.

The fortifications, which scarcely deserved the name, had taken little time to finish. Men and women of the village had pitched in to help, and only when their phase was finished had Stone sent them packing to the north, away from the converging enemy columns. With any luck, they were a mile or two away by now, and safe beyond the line of fire.

With any luck.

Speaking of luck, Stone could use some now, lying belly-down in the shallow trench he had cut, with help from two of the Laotian refugees, in the flimsy hut. The trench would keep him below the line of fire from gunners on the outside, but it might become his grave if they should torch the hut or drop grenades inside.

No matter. He had weighed the chances, gauged the risks, and now he was committed. There had been no time for more sophisticated planning or construction. Given what they had, the team had done their best.

Each one of them had picked a hut, and all of them were now concealed like Stone, tucked down in shallow trenches, eyes and guns alert along the firing slits cut hastily with machetes. They could move around to some degree inside the huts, commanding different fields of fire, but every move entailed the risk of rising from their trenches, exposing themselves to streams of automatic fire which could cut the shacks to pieces in a moment.

The whole plan was a gamble, but it was the best they had, the best that anyone could hope for on short notice, given the materials at hand. They had a chance—but only just. If everyone performed his duty, kept his head, then yes—they just might walk away from this alive.

And into what?

If they were not on time for their prearranged pickup, then what?

Stone closed his mind to that possibility, concentrating on the moment and its needs. Survival was the top priority, and that came one step at a time. This moment, here and now, took precedence over anything that might happen tomorrow, or even an hour in the future.

Stone was used to living on the edge, hanging on the moment, and he was not nervous now, but merely tense, keyed up, his nerves tingling in anticipation of the coming battle. If he could have seen the future—

Sudden movement at the limits of his peripheral vision, shifting underbrush along the eastern perimeter of the camp.

Stone brought his rifle closer, nosed its muzzle through the narrow aperture, aimed in the general direction of the target zone.

The undergrowth was parting there, a man emerging, dressed in mottled camouflage fatigues. Stone watched him as he cautiously began to circle, probing at the village's defenses, feeling out the night. The enemy was closing, and it was the Pathet Lao patrol. They were on time and moving in. Stone checked his watch and swore beneath his breath. No sign of their pursuers from the prison camp as yet. If they were forced to fight their battle piecemeal, it was finished. They could never hope to take two forces separately, when each was on alert and throwing its concerted weight behind the thrust.

Stone waited, breathed a silent prayer into the night, and eased the safety off. The time had come to improvise, and every second mattered now. Timing was everything. He had to do it right the first time, for there would never be a second chance on this side of the grave.

• • •

The hut reminded Jack Mandrell of prison, of the early days before the camp, when he and several others had been crowded into reeking huts, awaiting transport or the rough interrogation of their captors. He was sweating profusely, the palms of his hands slippery on the weapon that he held against his chest, stinging droplets of perspiration threatening to blind him when they fell into his eyes.

The others were all scattered: Stone away to his right, the Britisher somewhere behind him in the crude semicircular arrangement of the huts, the big one and his fellow prisoners together on his left. The rough arrangement gave them each a slightly different field of fire, and he rehearsed Mark Stone's instructions in his mind, making sure that he remembered them, forgetting nothing of importance.

It was a daring plan, no doubt about it, but the risks were terrible. Mandrell did not believe they had a chance, but at the moment that was not what bothered him.

It was confinement, lying in the sweltering darkness of the hut, which brought the cold sweat springing out of every pore. He was a free man, damn it, free at last, and there was no way in God's world that he was going back inside a cage. Not ever.

Except that now he lay inside a cage he had created for himself, and he was waiting for the enemy again, his very jailers, to emerge out of the trees and try to kill him.

Let them come. He would die before he let them take him back there, to that living hell. Mandrell had served his time, and then some. The bastards would have a dead man on their hands before they took him in again and caged him like a beast.

He saw the movement without recognizing it at first, and he was gaping at the opening in the trees when a human figure left the shadows, taking on substance. He recognized the Oriental features, the military garb, the weapon carried cautiously and at the ready. This was Pathet Lao, the animals who dropped by Mandrell's prison camp from time to time to banter with the damned Vietnamese and get their jollies out of kicking prisoners around. It was all that he could do to keep from jabbing his rifle through the makeshift firing slit and ripping off a burst right now, riddling the bastard where he stood.

But there was need for caution, and he waited, feeling his pulse increase, now hammering inside his head. His finger tightened on the trigger, and he had the target in his sights, just waiting for the signal that would let his hate and fear come spilling out, erupting through the muzzle of his weapon.

It was not time. The players weren't assembled yet. They were still waiting for another column, this one from the west, arriving any minute.

He wondered if the Pathet Lao would give them time to wait, and in the ringing stillness of his private cell, the P.O.W. realized he didn't give a damn.

Commander Chong Tri Minh was cursing underneath his breath, tripping over roots and rocks in the darkness. Every step was an ordeal, and the pounding in his chest was frightening. He had not felt such raw emotion since his first engagement in the Tet Offensive, when he matched his troops against American Marines.

There had been fear that day, and triumph. Now the fear was tempered with another sort of feeling—a sensation of impending doom that he could not shake off.

Commander Chong was not religious, certainly. His parents had been Buddhists, but he had renounced them, fingered them for Uncle Ho's police when the enlightenment came over him and he decided to make the Party and its military wing his life. The past was dead now, dead and buried. All that mattered was the present, and the future.

Chong's future, at the moment, seemed as dangerous and dismal as the forest all around him. They weren't gaining any ground to speak of in their hot pursuit, from what his eyes could tell him, and while they were certainly still on the track of their quarry, he had no way of telling how far behind they had fallen with the bungled river crossing and their other problems on the trail. He was pushing the men to their limit, aware that they must rest or break before much longer, but he didn't care. Stragglers would be shot, and all the others would take strength from their example. Chong would have his prey, or none of them were going back alive.

The sounds of firing up ahead alerted him at once, and he was thrashing through the undergrowth, moving forward rapidly along the column, when one of his scouts doubled back to report what they had heard. There was still some distance left to travel—perhaps two miles of rugged jungle track—but they were growing closer and the sounds of automatic firing, muffled by the forest, were a beacon that renewed Chong's own enthusiasm and the ardor of his troops.

They had a goal in sight now, or almost, and they redoubled their pace, no longer taking care to camouflage the noise they made in their passing. The enemy was up ahead, with more things on his mind than crackling twigs and branches in the jungle.

Chong did not waste his time trying to deduce what might be happening, who might have met the enemy, engaged him in a firefight. It was not important. All that mattered was the distance that he closed with every stride, the fact that he was growing closer to his quarry, to his self-redemption. There was still a chance of saving something from the grim fiasco of this day.

He cursed a lagger, slapped him hard across the face and

drove him onward, like an animal bound for market. Moving in the middle of the column, Chong had taken out insurance for himself in case of ambush—and he was in a position to watch out for any stragglers who might try to drop out of the chase.

Another mile, now less, and he would have them. Let the capitalist god have mercy on their souls.

Mark Stone was getting nervous now, no doubt about it. Several moments had elapsed since he caught sight of the invader, moving cautiously inside the camp, and now the guy was gesturing behind him, calling up the reinforcements. Other figures were emerging from the darkness of the forest, merging into groups of two and three as they advanced, fanning out into a pincer movement.

Stone was watching as their point man reached the nearest hut and kicked it in, dropping to a crouch as he ducked through the doorway, rifle at the ready. He had picked an empty that time, but the game was getting too damned close to call, and Stone expected uninvited company at any moment, slamming through the door and throwing down on him with automatic weapons.

They were out of time, and he could feel the pieces of his plan collapsing all around him, fractured images, spinning in a grim kaleidoscope of death. They didn't have a choice now; when the Pathet Lao discovered them, they had to fight, whether the Viets arrived to make it work or not.

And it would never work unless they *did* arrive.

Stone cursed again and tightened up his finger on the CAR-15's trigger. Thirty paces out, in front of him, the point man was emerging from the empty hut and moving straight for Stone's, carrying his rifle with a sort of easy caution. Just another moment, maybe two, and Stone would have to start the ball without the guests of honor.

The Laotian was perhaps a dozen yards away and closing

when he halted and swiveled to the west, swinging his weapon up instinctively. Stone followed the direction of his adversary's eyes, and saw a group of men emerging from the forest on the far side of the little village. One of them had a hand upraised—in warning or in greeting—and he was about to call out something to the Lao guerrillas, either hailing them or calling out for some sort of ID.

Either way, he never got the chance. Stone saw his opening and didn't hesitate, already tracking as he recognized the uniforms of the Vietnamese regulars.

He squeezed off his initial burst at the new arrivals, leveling a pair of them and sweeping the Viet point man away into the darkened jungle. Suddenly, a score of weapons opened up in ragged concert, and hell was visiting the tiny jungle village for the second time in a few hours.

Stone kept firing, choosing targets carefully, selectively, aware of other weapons firing from the huts on either side of him. They were playing this one for all the marbles, but at least they had a chance. With any luck at all, it would be chance enough.

Chapter Twenty-one

Stone milked another burst out of his CAR-15 and watched a Pathet Lao commando go down, writhing on the hard-packed soil of the jungle clearing. The guy was still alive and screaming out the final moments of his life, and Stone left him to it, tracking on in search of other, more worthy targets.

All around the little village, automatic weapons tore the midnight apart, Vietnamese and Pathet Lao firing back and forth at one another, each side convinced that it had engaged the enemy, had been betrayed by someone in the opposition ranks.

And it was working like a charm, beyond Stone's wildest hope. The trap was sprung with all his enemies inside, and it was working.

Except that he and all his men were in the middle of the trap. And it was time to give some serious thought to getting out of there, in one hellacious hurry, before the savvy hostiles tumbled to his ruse and formed a strong united front against the common adversary.

Time to pull out, damned right, but it was easier said than done.

Stone wriggled up and out of his slit trench, crawling belly-down across the earthen floor with bullets eating up the air above his head. Both sides were pouring fire into the huts, taking fire from his commandos in return, no one certain who it was inside there, laying down the cover fire. Each side would think the other had arrived before it to set the trap, and each side was reacting with an all-out effort to destroy the village.

Stone had made it as far as the doorway when a body hit the flimsy door and tumbled through. He had perhaps a heartbeat to recognize the face and uniform as Pathet Lao, and then the gunner saw him and swiveled up and out of his awkward sprawl, bringing his weapon to bear on the unexpected enemy with swift professionalism.

Stone beat him to it, putting a round into his left eye at a range of less than fifteen feet, lifting the top of his skull in a gray-pink spray. The almost headless body rolled away, and Stone was past it in an instant, moving smoothly toward the open doorway, reloading on the move. Outside, the jungle night was lit flickeringly by muzzle blasts, and he was racing right into it, to join the dance.

Jack Mandrell ejected the empty magazine from his Kalashnikov and slammed a new one—his last—into the smoking receiver of his assault rifle. He had emptied two full loads already, dropping a dozen soldiers on both sides, and he was on a roll. Adrenaline was pumping through his system, taking him on to a high that he remembered from the days in 'Nam, before he had been captured in the final stages of a covert border raid.

Mandrell also had been a Green Beret, and there was no

forgetting some of the training they had received at Bragg and elsewhere. It was in his blood, just like the love of being free, the hatred for the animals who had locked him up and treated him like so much garbage.

He rolled up and out of his protective trench, no longer satisfied at firing from a safe position, anxious to be out there in the middle of the killing, doing his own share to cut the odds. A bullet grazed his shoulder, rocking him backward, but he faced the sudden blaze of pain with equanimity, a smile etched deep into his facial muscles.

Despite his weakness, he was living. For the first time in a goddamned decade, adrenaline made him feel the life inside him again, and nothing short of death would slow him down this time. He found his feet, ignoring other bullets as they punctured flimsy walls and roof, tugging at his clothing, drawing blood from wounds he never felt.

He made it through the doorway to surprise a squat Vietnamese who was attempting to find shelter in the shadows there. The gunner spun to face him, but he never had a chance with Mandrell's weapon leveled at his face. The three-round burst left his body sprawling almost headless in the dust.

Mandrell sucked in a deep lungful of clear night air, relishing the smell of gunsmoke. He was flying, soul no longer earthbound, finally free of all restraints, and nothing could have made him any happier unless it was to see...

Commander Chong!

Jack Mandrell saw the short Vietnamese officer through a swirl of battlesmoke and knew him in an instant. Just a heartbeat's hesitation, grinding his knuckles into his eyes to remove the possibility of hallucination, and he looked again, confirming the first ID.

It was Commander Chong, the very bastard who had made his life a hell these past eight years, the rotten sonofabitch who had mutilated Alex Bradford as a punishment for his escape attempt, the slimy piece of filth who had derived so much perverse enjoyment from the grim captivity of others, making every day an endless nightmare.

Mandrell was moving through the middle of the battle-field, unmindful of the gunfire around him, hearing voices calling to him to get down, to seek cover, but they didn't understand the sudden urgency he felt, the *need* that was as real as the need for oxygen.

Chong saw him coming, but couldn't quite believe his eyes. The little Asian drew his pistol, leveled it unsteadily in the direction of his former prisoner, and Jack Mandrell unleashed a blazing figure-eight that took him in the knees, exploding bone and cartilage to drop him backward on his ass.

The little shit was screaming something Jack Mandrell would never understand, but he could get the gist of it, all right. He read the pain and desperation in the keening voice, and knew that Chong was finally finding himself on the receiving end of all the hell he had dished out across the years.

It was a start, but it was damn sure not enough to satisfy Mandrell. Not yet.

He saw a figure rushing toward him from the left, bayonet stretched out ahead of him like a jousting lance. Jack pivoted and let him have a three-round burst that opened up his belly like a rotten grain sack. The corpse reeled on for half a dozen strides, then folded over and collapsed onto the bloody ground, unmoving.

And he turned his full attention back to Chong. The captain was enveloped in his pain, unmindful of the pistol lying almost close enough to reach. Mandrell half-wished that he would try for it, that he would make it easy, but a part of him was happy that the camp commander was un-armed. He had another sort of treat in store for Chong before he let him find the sweet release of death.

Mandrell was on him now, slinging the AK-47 over his shoulder on its leather sling, reaching down to grab the squat Vietnamese beneath his arms. He started half-dragging, half-carrying the captain, making sure his shattered legs made contact with the ground at every lurching stride. Chong's screams were music to his ears, eclipsing everything else, drowning out the sound of automatic weapons all around them.

And he never heard the second trooper coming, never saw the flash of firelight on the bayonet before it plunged into his back at kidney level.

Mandrell died standing up, without ever really comprehending what had happened to him, toppling forward at the final moment, sprawling out across the wounded captain's shattered legs. That wrenched another scream from Chong, and Jack Mandrell was smiling as he slipped into the blackness with it ringing in his ears, a distant melody of sweet revenge.

Mark Stone saw the P.O.W. die, and ripped a burst into his killer, spiraling out of it to let the wounded prison camp commander have his share. And then there was no time for Stone to think about them, to lament the passing of a prisoner named Jack Mandrell, because the war was coming to him with a vengeance.

The night dissolved into a string of grim, firelit scenarios that would be emblazoned on his mind forever. Stone was choosing targets, killing, dodging slugs that sought him in return.

And he saw Hog Wiley, reeling through the battle smoke with his carbine in hand. Alex Bradford rode his back like a child at play, both arms wrapped around his thick neck, legs about his waist, and the remaining P.O.W., Wilcox, had a weapon now, using it with grim determination as he watched their flank.

Terrance Loughlin, on the other side of the encampment, was just emerging now from the hut that had sheltered him, diving into a shoulder roll as two snipers tried to throw down on him simultaneously. He came up, still rolling, still weaving, and he got them both, his automatic weapon flinging out a deadly one-two punch that blew them both away.

And all around them, Pathet Lao and Vietnamese were busy killing and being killed, slaughtering each other in the confusion of the firefight. Those who saw the Westerners among them, those who realized the trap and recognized its danger, did not live to sound the general warning. They were busy dying, anywhere and everywhere that Stone and his companions found them and dug them out.

Everywhere the smell of death and burning was oppressive, omnipresent, choking the nostrils and clogging the senses until it became everything, an end and a beginning.

Stone emptied out his weapon and reloaded, emptied it again. The field was littered with his kills and those of his companions, bodies lying frozen in the attitudes of sudden, violent death.

He saw Lan Vang, machete in hand, astride the body of a Pathet Lao commando, slashing furiously at the mutilated corpse, a grimace of intense concentration on his oval face. He caught Stone's eye, flashed a quick thumbs-up, and bent again to his task with renewed vigor.

Out of nowhere, a Vietnamese was on the little guide, his own knife rising and falling in the firelight. Stone moved closer, trying for a shot, but the two of them were locked together, tussling, no quarter asked or given. Both of them were wounded and bleeding heavily, but neither would surrender, keeping up the frenzied thrashing as they rolled in the direction of the nearest hut and finally sprawled inside the open doorway.

Stone was closing on it when the hut exploded, something

inside having been detonated by a bullet or grenade. The hut collapsed into fiery ruin, the concussion driving him backward and away. He grimaced, turned away from there, and went on about the business of his war.

It required a moment for Mark Stone to recognize the sudden, ringing stillness. In a moment, almost before he recognized the fact, all firing ceased, and nothing else disturbed the silence of the village save the hungry hiss of flames in thatch behind him. Scanning, searching for some sign of life, he found Hog and his charges, then picked out Loughlin, rising from the shadow of another nearby shanty. The CAR-15 dangled from one hand, his smoking Browning autoloader in the other.

And they were all alive, after all. Except for Jack Mandrell. They came together in the center of the destroyed village, exchanging glances that spoke silent volumes, sharing that brief moment. Stone explained the other prisoner's fate in solemn tones, and added what had happened to their guide in the last moments of the conflict.

"That's too damned bad," Hog said, with genuine emotion in his gravel voice. "I kinda liked him."

Wilcox cleared his throat and asked, "Can we find our way out without him?"

"No sweat," Hog answered. "We're damn near home already."

A strained smile passed around the little circle, living warriors grinning in the face of death, and Stone jerked his thumb to the east, where dawn was threatening to set the sky afire.

"We'd better get a move on, then," he told them all. "We've got a flight to catch."

"With pleasure," Loughlin told him.

"Lemme at those friendly skies," Hog beamed.

They turned as one, and moved away from there, into

the dawn, where Meyers and Hopkins still waited with the Huey that would take them out of that hellhole. The jungle closed behind them, blotting out the traces of their passage as if man had never passed that way and never would.

Epilogue

The jungle waits. It lives and breathes; it shelters secrets. Somewhere in its vastness, huddled in their cages, eyes turned skyward at each sound of planes or helicopters, other captives swelter in the hell that has become routine. Where consciousness remains, where sanity has clung in shadowed corners, they remember . . . and they wait.

For tomorrow. For the next day. For sometime.

Someone must remember, come for them, expunge a people's debt of guilt and gratitude.

Perhaps one man. One dedicated man, determined to repay that debt whatever obstacles may be erected in his way. A warrior of the old breed, more devoted to his honor and his duty than to mere convenience and expediency.

Someday. One day.

And still they wait.

SPECIAL PREVIEW

Here are some scenes from

CAMBODIAN HELLHOLE

second novel in the exciting M.I.A. HUNTER series

coming from Jove in April!

Terrance Loughlin waited in the darkness, alone, watching the compound below him, counting down the heartbeats to oblivion.

They were still on schedule, from what he could see, and true night was only ninety minutes old. Plenty of time left yet to accomplish the mission and get back out again before the first light of dawn burned off the morning fog and left them vulnerable.

He scanned the dark line of the river, taking several seconds to pick out the form of Hog Wiley, knowing, even as he did so, exactly where the giant of a man should be. Lon Ky and two of the Hmong warriors were accompanying him, clinging tight against the shoreline, taking full advantage of the darkness and the undergrowth. They were in position now, almost opposite the drainage pipe where Stone had made his own ill-fated entry to the compound more than twenty-four hours earlier.

Loughlin had warned them about the sentries in the drain-

pipe, and about the charge he had planted especially for
their amusement. He saw now that Hog and the others were
giving the pipe a wide enough berth; when it went up, they
should not be caught in the backblast, unless they strayed
from their present places of concealment.

One Hmong was missing, and Loughlin glanced away
to the west, knowing he could never pick the man out in
the stygian darkness of the rain forest. He would be in place
by now, armed and ready to create the diversion they were
all counting on him for. Another moment now, perhaps
less . . .

As if on cue, an automatic rifle opened up across the
wide part of the river, near the end of the bridge. Its muzzle
flashes, unconcealed, were dirty orange and brilliant against
the shrubbery and trees.

Bullets started thunking into the gate of the compound,
drilling neat lines of holes through the bamboo fencing.
Voices inside were beginning to shout, some of them seeking information, others clearly barking orders, as the defenders tried to think of some acceptable response to the
challenge.

A rifle was thrust through a slit in the bamboo fence,
followed immediately by another, and they began stroking
off wild bursts in the direction of the treeline. It would have
been a miracle if they hit anything but empty air.

Another moment, and the front gate was opening, exactly
as Loughlin had hoped it might, and a squad of perhaps a
dozen uniformed men came pouring out, led by a noncom
who brandished a sidearm and fired it every third step or
so, aiming toward the Hmong troopers' moving, twinkling
muzzle flashes. They were closing fast. Loughlin let them
make it to the midpoint of the bridge before he raised his
little radio-remote detonator box, fingering the fire control
button.

Below him, at river level, things began going to hell in a hurry.

The bridge supports blew out with half a dozen smoky thunderclaps, and then the whole bridge turned into a crumbling, rolling lane of fire. Soldiers—and parts of them— were airborne, some of them screaming out the last fractured seconds of their worthless lives, the rest already far beyond the spoken word. Bits and pieces of the bridge and its occupants were thudding down along the bank or splashing in the stream and raising little frothy geysers.

Loughlin did not wait for the shock of that initial blast to wear off. Swiveling where he sat, he keyed another button on the detonator's master panel, touching off the secondary charges.

The drainpipe went first, instantly consumed in fire that devoured its squatting sentries in their tunnel, before they had a chance to register the shaking of the earth beneath their feet. One instant they were there; the next, they might never have existed.

Finally the charges he had set against the southern fenced perimeter went off in unison, blasting through the stand of bamboo, clearing Hog and the Hmong an entry the size of a double doorway at a posh hotel. He saw them up and at it, moving before the smoke and falling debris had a chance to clear away.

And Loughlin was on the move himself now, dropping the exhausted detonator where he was and picking up the CAR-15 assault rifle that had been lying on the damp earth beside him. He slithered down the slope, fairly crashing through the underbrush, no longer taking care to keep his movements silent. The defenders over there had plenty on their minds and on their hands without worrying about some twigs cracking in the forest now, some sixty yards away. They could not see him, could not hear him—but the Britisher meant to change all that, and very soon.

He was closing in for the kill, determined to be a part of the final confrontation with the camp's defense. Loughlin had already done his part by closing off the bridge and opening the camp, by wiping out a dozen of the soldiers who would otherwise oppose them now, but he did not intend to be left out of the action after coming so far and risking so much to be a part of it.

He reached the river and waded out into the frigid water, holding his assault rifle overhead to keep it dry. It was difficult to move quickly, but he did his best, forsaking the avenue of entry used by Wiley and the Hmong. The open gate was closer, and he moved toward it obliquely, passing bits of floating rubble from the bridge, and bits of bodies, torn and blackened, floating on the surface.

Another hundred feet now . . . seventy-five . . .

He braced himself for the assault and redoubled his pace, already smelling battle smoke and blood, hearing the gunshots and the cries of the wounded and dying.

Loughlin was home at last.

Kneeling, wrists bound with rope behind his back, Stone waited for another blow to fall. They had been battering him for almost an hour now, and he was dizzy, aching, on the verge of losing consciousness.

He knew that if he crumbled, sprawled out on the floor, the camp commander would find some way of reviving him and going on with the interrogation. The Vietnamese officer was almost frantic now, pacing back and forth in front of Stone, fairly shouting his questions, snapping at his guards when it was time to do some clubbing with their weighted canes. And if they did not set about it fast enough to suit him, he would slap them, brushing them aside to punch or kick at Stone himself.

Any moment now, Stone told himself. It could not be

much longer. They were out there, waiting for the time to strike.

"Where are your accomplices?" the commander shrieked, his lips almost in Mark Stone's face. "Tell me where they are!"

Stone dredged up a smile from the bottom of his soul and said, "Fuck you."

A hard boot landed in his ribs, and then all three of the Vietnamese were wading in, knocking him off balance, driving him to the rough floorboards of the command hut. He tried to roll himself in a protective fetal curl, but the arms bound behind his back were giving him trouble, making it hard for him to protect either kidneys or ribs.

There was a sudden burst of automatic weapons fire, somewhere outside the camp, and his three assailants backed off instantly, poised and listening.

It was beginning.

Another burst, more sustained, and now, before the commandant could issue any orders, weapons from inside the camp were answering, firing blindly into the outer darkness.

The captain looked down at him hatefully, seemed about to kick him in the stomach, then decided that there was no time to waste on entertainment. He moved toward the door, one of his orderlies falling into step behind him, peering through the window before he went outside, as if to make sure the attackers were not already waiting for him on his doorstep.

Finally satisfied, he went out on the covered porch, calling to his men in the yard, getting responses, issuing more orders in a singsong, cracking voice. Within a minute he was back inside the CP hut, leaving the door open at his back, revealing a wedge-shaped slice of darkness, prison cages in the background.

"A feeble attempt," he told Stone, trying to gloat and not quite achieving his goal. "My men will deal with your riflemen in short order, now that we know their position."

Riflemen? What the hell?

Before the grim interrogation could resume, Stone heard the telltale sounds of a small patrol racing out of the camp, their voices growing marginally smaller in the direction of the footbridge.

And suddenly their voices and everything else were swallowed by the roar of rapid-fire explosions, ripping the night apart, sending tremors through the ground on which the stilted CP shack was standing.

The camp commander paled, losing all of his color in the space of a heartbeat, looking for all the world like a man instantly drained of blood. He glared at Stone, then raced in the direction of the doorway, his orderly not on his heels. Over his shoulder he barked a single order to the trooper who remained behind.

Stone had learned enough Vietnamese in his tours of Asian duty to translate an order for his own death. The soldier was moving briskly, turning away from him, heading for the corner of the shack where two AK-47s stood, propped together carelessly.

It was now or never, and to hell with all the aches and pains that wracked his body. Stone would find his feet and move, or he would die amost immediately. It was that simple.

He rolled over onto his back, clenching his teeth and biting off the groan that forced itself into his tortured throat. Curling himself into yet a tighter ball, he bent his legs at the knees, ankles tight together, sitting up until he could reach his heels with his hands. That accomplished, it took perhaps another second for him to slip his feet through the loop of rope that bound his hands together, bringing his hands around in front of him again, where they would be some use for fighting.

He struggled to his feet, lurching, staggering, and the

gunner was well ahead of him now, already bending down
to close one hand around the barrel of an automatic rifle.
Stone took two shambling steps, then launched himself into
a headlong tackle, his forehead and shoulder striking the
human target low, in the small of his back, and driving him
face-first against the wall.

They fell together, the guard more stunned and surprised
than Stone for an instant. Blood was streaming down his
face where his nose had smashed against the wall of the CP
hut, and he was shaking his head to clear it, dabbing at the
blood with one hand, groping with the other for his weapon.

And outside, more smoky thunder tore the night, this
time from the south side—it was a section of the fence
being blown away.

Stone was behind his enemy, the taut rope between his
wrists serving as an admirable garrote now, biting deep into
the orderly's throat, closing off his airway, dragging his
head back and chafing the flesh until more rivulets of crimson stained his khaki uniform. A final twist, the snap of
separating vertebrae, and he was still.

Stone found a knife in the guard's pocket, opened it, and
finally freed his hands with difficulty. Satisfied that they
would serve him, he picked up the rifle that his late opponent
had been scrambling for so desperately. He racked the cock-
ing lever back, chambering a round, and eased the safety
off.

A hurtling body cleared the doorway, skidding to a stop.
It was the second orderly, returning for the rifle that he had
forgotten in his haste to get outside.

Stone let him see the weapon in his hands, let him watch
the muzzle tracking into target acquisition, and then he blew
the scum away, putting a short five-round burst dead center
in his chest, propelling him backward through the open
doorway and out into the smoky night.

Stone followed him out, moving on shaky legs at first,

rapidly gathering strength from the sounds and sights of combat, savoring the rich aroma of the killing ground. It was the medicine he needed now, this moment, and with any luck at all, it would be enough to see him through a walk into hell and back again.

Hog Wiley led his band of warriors through the smoking breach in the prison camp's bamboo fence, with Lon Ky hot on his heels. The other men were peeling off, each closing on his assigned target, nailing down the guards who posed the greatest threat to the P.O.W.'s, but Wiley hung back a moment, scanning the scene of orchestrated chaos with narrowed eyes.

First and foremost, he was looking for Stone. Failing in that objective, he was trying to get a rough estimate of hostile strength, their general deployment, before he committed his tiny force to some action that might prove suicidal.

Before Hog had a chance to finish up his instant recon, a gunner in the western guard tower spotted him, swung his light machine gun around, and sent a lethal hailstorm in the Texan's general direction. Slugs were eating up the ground around his feet, and Hog went into a diving shoulder roll, loosing a quick burst from his assault rifle as he made the move.

Coming up in a combat crouch, he stroked another burst into the tower, and saw his bullets harmlessly deflected by the heavier logs its builders had used to line the fortified, exposed position. Cursing, he quickly set the rifle down, unlimbering the LAW rocket launcher he wore slung across his back like a quiver full of arrows.

One deadly arrow, this one, ready to pierce the heart of his attacker's crude defenses.

Hog yanked the pin and primed the launcher, swinging it up onto his shoulder and sighting on the guard tower in one practiced motion born of long experience with martial tools. He hit the firing lever and watched the rustling firebird climb away from him, rattling toward its target on a comet-tail of flame.

The machine-gunner saw it coming, but there was no place for him to go, and no damned time to get there. The tower detonated like an ammo dump on stilts, spewing chunks of burning logs and blackened flesh over the breadth of the compound.

Over by the cages, Hog could see the two Hmong troopers who had accompanied him already blasting locks off the bamboo cages, freeing some of the prisoners inside, using their automatic weapons to repulse a halfhearted counterattack by the camp's defenders.

It was early yet, and the Vietnamese required a little time to recover from the initial shock of the assault, to put their defense together and get it in good working order. It was Wiley's job to see that they never got the time they needed.

A pair of gunners in the east tower, on his right, were firing down into the compound now, indiscriminately, trying for anything and everything at once. Their wild rounds were impacting near the cages, scattering the Hmong, even driving their own troops back into cover for a moment.

Hog saw Lon Ky appear from nowhere, marching directly toward the guard tower, firing his AK-47 from the hip like a little movie gangster going in for the showdown. He was peppering the target, spending his whole magazine—and getting no more positive results than Wiley had with the first tower.

The chief gunner stood up, standing his weapon almost on its nose to bring the Cambodian guerrilla under fire. The first long burst took off Lon Ky's head at the shoulders, leaving him standing like a headless mannequin before another burst of slugs cut him off at the knees and blew him backward, out of the action completely.

Cursing, Wiley ripped a thermite grenade from his web harness, jerked the pin free, and let it fly in a looping overhand. He was rewarded as the lethal egg dropped squarely on target, directly into the open lookout tower, slightly behind the machine-gun emplacement.

A heartbeat passed while the gunner tried to find him, and his loader tried to find out what had fallen in among them—then the night was turned to instant noon by the detonation of the incendiary charge. Glowing coals of thermite fanned across the compound, setting fires wherever they touched down, enveloping the tower—or what was left of it—in dense white smoke.

Before the smoke obscured everything, Hog had a glimpse of the gunner, still at his weapon, hands fused to the metal now, screaming out his life as the coals ate into him and through him, unquenchable by blood or any other human fluids.

Wiley left them to it, turning back into the compound proper, holding his assault rifle at the ready as he moved out, hunting. He would find Mark Stone, alive or dead. Without him, Wiley did not plan to leave himself. They went together or they stayed together. Simple.